George Elliott Clarke is an award-winning poet,
playwright and screenwriter. He is the author of
six collections of poetry and a winner of the
Governor General's Award in 2001. A seventh-
generation African Canadian, Clarke was born
in Windsor, Nova Scotia, near the community of
Three Mile Plains. He is an associate professor
of English at the University of Toronto.

GEORGE ELLIOTT CLARKE

George & Rue

VINTAGE BOOKS
London

Published by Vintage 2006

2 4 6 8 10 9 7 5 3 1

First published in Canada in 2005 by
HarperCollins Publishers Ltd

First published in Great Britain in 2005 by
The Harvill Press

Vintage
Random House, 20 Vauxhall Bridge Road,
London SW1V 2SA

Random House Australia (Pty) Limited
20 Alfred Street, Milsons Point, Sydney,
New South Wales 2061, Australia

Random House New Zealand Limited
18 Poland Road, Glenfield, Auckland 10, New Zealand

Random House (Pty) Limited
Isle of Houghton, Corner of Boundary Road & Carse O'Gowrie,
Houghton, 2198, South Africa

Random House Publishers India Private Limited
301 World Trade Tower, Hotel Intercontinental Grand Complex,
Barakhamba Lane, New Delhi 110 001, India

The Random House Group Limited Reg. No. 954009
www.randomhouse.co.uk/vintage

A CIP catalogue record for this book
is available from the British Library

SBN 9780099485179 (from Jan 2007)
ISBN 0099485176

Papers used by Random House are natural,
recyclable products made from wood grown in
sustainable forests. The manufacturing processes
conform to the environmental regulations of the
country of origin

Printed and bound in Great Britain by
Bookmarque Ltd, Croydon, Surrey

DISCLAIMER

Though based on several actual persons and one actual crime, this novel employs facts not found in mere trial transcripts— the scratchy songs, the mouthed bits from blues. George and Rufus Hamilton always lived outside boundaries (including knowledge, including history, including archives). They are "encompassed" here only by unrestrained imagination. That is the only truth in this novel, whose English ain't broken, but "blackened."

For Geraldine Elizabeth Clarke (1939–2000),
David Johnson,
Joan Mendes,
and Angus "Sock" Johnson:
four siblings of Three Mile Plains, Nova Scotia.

For William Lloyd Clarke,
artist, of Halifax, Nova Scotia.

And for Geeta,
indomitable intellectual,
wilful wife.

Un être absent de sa beauté est deux fois plus beau.
—VIOLETTE LEDUC

What avails it to recall Beauty back to us?
—COUNTEE CULLEN

A WHITE devil moon haunts the black 1949 brand-new four-door Ford sedan when a black hammer slip out a pocket and smuck the taxi driver's head, from the side. Not just a knock-out blow, the hammer was a landslide of iron. It crashed down unnervingly.

It'd been a turny road, sliding all over, where they'd been, outside Fredericton—cold, colourless city—on January 7th, 1949. The moon's whiteness was cold—some pure hydrochloric acid blackening pines and spruce. Bad nerves, inconsiderate nerves, a jittering hand got that hammer smashing down. Its wielder couldn't see straight; it was like his head was sunk underwater. The hunger in his gut was, he figured, much worse than any maybe pain he did. The slugged guy's breath was a groan that almost drowned out the radio glowing with night's crooners. The hand that'd held the hammer now dropped it clunkily on the floor. As far as the hitter knew, he'd scored moolah, a real win-win situation for any True Crime fan. (In funny papers, people who aren't made of steel are made of water: nothing hurts them. Strike a man with a hammer and he just gets a big white bump on his head and jumps up and slugs you with a bigger hammer.)

Sick of his victim's moans, the double-dealing passenger picked up the hammer and clipped the man again. Hard, bloody action. The struck-down man breathed less and less—like he was calmly asleep. Not right in the eye of God, it was, but the batterer didn't feel shameful or dirty. There was blood splashed on his face and clothes, blood all over the car seat, and black blood on the dying man's face. The car floor was sticky with blood; stains speckled the window.

Moonlight daggered into that country 'n' western radio car as if to zero in on this crime scene. The fare began to think about rifling the zonked man's pockets, stabbing into them to haul out coins, bills. The bond between him and the snoozing man was a wound. Then the front door snapped open and another man appeared, a dark silhouette: Soon, two men feasted on the taxi driver's property.

WHIP

If something is not done, we shall be the murderers of our children.

—THOMAS JEFFERSON

I

ASA FUMBLED in his shirt for a cigarette; the sweet vice he needed with a new un being born. He sure loathed the fact of a fourth mouth now. Christmas 1926 hovered like an Angel of Destruction. Winter was the stench of oil lugged home. Or it was lugging snow into the kitchen to make tea. Or it was trying to battle oppressive rain, that forceful misery soaking up the newspapered floor. Or it was a crop of rats. The sloughs were laced with ice; a crust of crystal formed in the waterpail. And no bite of even bad meat anywhere. Flour bags got scissored and sewn into shirts, bleached underwear got milled from the Five Roses flour company. They had to make bread using potato water instead of milk.

Asa'd had enough. Now Cynthy got the new un comin, comin, her screams scarin even crows off the night-blackening fields. Where was the slow-as-cold-molasses midwife already? Him was tired, Cynthy was wore out.

Asa went back into the shack to give Cynthy the wooden spoonhandle to clench. He found it and put it between her gritting, gnashing teeth. He wet a cloth at the washstand and dabbed the sweat on her brow. Him say, "Ain't no fuss, now, Cinthee. Alisha be here soon; keep calm." She took his big, scarred, rough hand in hers, and nodded. She was pure pretty, with her tan face and waist-length black hair, part Mi'kmaq Negress, and her eyes sweet like rum. She grunted, smiled, nodded, the big quilt humped up over her belly, beautiful-beautiful.

Asa looked away. Why did birth hurt so? Because it was the first proof life'd go hard. Times the baby come out and the mother just droops dead; times both of em perish; times the baby sighs, dies, and the mother just gets bigged up again. At least two-year-old Georgie was up his grandfolks' up Green Street. Good God. One less trouble tonight.

Asa walked out the back room and to the front door. Look like Alisha, the conjure woman, proachin now. Clip-clop of horse hooves percolatin down the hill ferryin a black shape cloaked up blackly against the pooling gloom. It be Alisha, for sure: thin scarecrow-witch shape, old pointy face. That same moment, Asa look askance at Alisha cause he's a-scared of her. Her face is so ugly, Asa thinks her mama could've been jailed for keeping a private dump.

But Alisha don't care for no man: can any man equal the power and grace of a woman delivering new life, just nine months from the start and all set to go? A man bossin a woman be silly; Alisha see, it's the woman who take all the risk in the business and who make all the profit. What some man bring to it but a big mouth and a bigger gut?

And who could doctor like her? She'd served chicken-shit tea to remedy ulcers, whisky tea to carry away a chill. (This remedy'd make ya feel sweaty, dizzy, and good.) She also conjured up sarsaparilla for colds, tansy for arthritis, camel's root for thrush, and burdock leaves for fever. She made tonics for measles, and boiled roots, herbs, to doctor the mumps. She stuck rickety babies in warm water to straighten out their bones. Healing needed only cow-turd plasters, fumes of lime, and spoonfuls of molasses. She could deliver Cynthy's chile, convictedly a boy, with no fuss a-tall. Unless God drove things different.

Cynthy screamed again. "Christ Almighty, it's comin!"

And then Alisha, busy, sable wasp, was there, leapin off the horse, tossin the reins to Asa who finally had something he could do, and she be bustlin—warm, loud—into the yellow-lit kitchen, then into the back room, with the muddy newspaper floor, rats hidin, waitin for the light to fail, and with Cynthy moanin, rockin, buckin. Alisha set down her big black doctor's bag, brimming with her own homemade magic as well as the sterile items Dr. Keddy give her. (The doc travelled by horse and wagon, Alisha only by horse.) Alisha pulled up a stool beside Cynthy and commenced her salvation work. She prayed. She manipulated. She prodded. She fussed.

Cynthy moaned and sang, "Sweet Jesus, Sweeeeet Jesus, Sweeeeeeeet, Christ, Sweeeeeeeet Jeeeeeesus."

Asa heard the cries, but started to drool, thinkin of rum.

Smoking, Asa looked up at the smoked-out stars. He thought of Cynthy Croxen the way she was when she and he was in love way back then. Her ebon, chestnut hair, her onyx and honey eyes, her Black Watch tartan skirt, her legs—smooth as cool wood, her red-brown skin, just her overpowering beauty down by Gibsons Woods, that oasis of nice-looking people who were always throwing all-night parties. He'd snatched her up to him right there, at a dance, harmonica blazing and fiddle sizzling and too much rhythmic clapping. He'd not been fortified with a beer when his eyes caught, snagged, on that dreamy face, too alarmingly splendid. Blossoms were just jettisoning off the apple trees in pastures up, down, the Annapolis Valley—fifty miles of apple blossoms, sir, pink-white-ivory-cream-rose blossoms, delicate to look at, fragile to touch, and the dance was in a barn just off some tan man's pasture. Blossoms was a-crizzle on the trees. Cynthy'd not said no when he'd up and asked her to dance. So he took her up—small as she was, light, well, light like light—and twirled her about the impromptu dance floor, some planks flung down among the stacked hay, some lamps for light, some beer for flavour, and some apple blossoms for scent. His hand on her waist, ah, it was like holding a plate of petals. They danced. They got all hugged up in a corner. Cynthy was sheathed light: her skin was sheer copper-brass-gold.

Later, four cream oxen, shimmering in spic-and-span moonlight, shimmied a cart over a puddle-pocked dirt road, nearby the squalls of apple blossoms, squabbles of pear blossoms. Cynthy's dress rustled like a Bible page. She looked a gold-leaf Cleopatra, smelled of Noxzema and Pond's. Asa took up Cynthy's light hand and kissed her fingers where they sat, trundled along in the cart. She looked at him, her eyes glinting as arrogant and soft as wine; then she smiled, and it was as beautiful as the moon. Her beauty was pure sugar in his mouth.

In 1923, Cynthy was sixteen and Asa was twenty-one. They went to a preacher and got attached forthwith. Asa sayin to his wife: "You lookin good in that wedding ring." The ring was only silver. Still, the dew of his kisses upon her made her own kisses wetter and freer. The only thing she wore was sunlight. They sipped Demerara rum then, then supped madly on each other. In the morning, she'd put her face on, Asa'd put the coffee on. They served each other breakfast in bed every day that first summer. The bedsprings screeched like church organs. There was hot biscuits, slabs of bacon. They buttered each other up sweetly-sweetly, gobbled each other down hotly-hotly. In each other, they had a little heaven, briefly. Maybe fried mackerel and buckwheat pancakes and berries for Sunday breakfast, maybe buttermilk and brown bread and blackstrap molasses—"bread and lally"—for Sunday supper. Now, a tall jug of ice water on the table beside the steaming-hot plates; later, a small dish of ice water on the floor beside the sweating-hot bed. Asa like the kind of love where the lovers get all sweaty.

There's just one thing, you gotta understand.
I say, there be just one thing, y'all mus understand:
It takes a lovin woman to make a lovin man.

Asa loved seeing pretty-pretty Cynthy's raining dark hair flying
like a horse's, and he loved their bucking, their breaking into
hoarse pants, her ebony hair flogging breath, lovely, satisfying,
and fresh, her lips blushing, sobbing moans, her serious mouth,
her ginger hips, his delirious charging, charging. Dependin on
light, she was tawny and mahogany and dusky and chocolate
and coffee and coconut and brass and bronze and rosy. Blackness were wine, muscles, sweat, laughter, fire, gleams, amen.
Cynthy'd slide into bed, eager to touch; Asa stiffened, became
hard to break. Asa felt love rising up like sugar rising in the
maples. He could quaff her kiss like milk with a fine relish, like a
fresh pan of milk instinct with honey. They'd get down in the
bed and fuck, and fuck, and fuck. Cynthy's kisses were burning
liquor. So sweet as the sweat that sugar makes as rum. His lips
emphasized her gold hips, her apple breasts.

That first year, Cynthy and Asa ate just three foods for three
months: mackerel, bread, and rum. Only peril was, for the newlyweds, potatoes sometimes substitute for rum. Asa could've
eaten a burlap sack full of cod or mackerel or herring, just by
himself. But food was really secondary, when all they felt they
needed was love and fresh water.

Asa figured his bestest possession be Cynthy, his wife, and
wouldn't it be nice to see such pleasure bear fruit? But at first,
after conjunction, she'd crush seeds of Queen Anne's lace, mix
the white powder with water, and drink to keep the babies off.
Still, who can forever refuse natural consequences of love?
And so, Georgie happened along. Same time last year, 1925.

That's when the sweetness turned ugly, with a squalling
baby, an often sick—and sickening—wife, and that was when

Asa started to feel they was the accursed of Three Mile Plains. But they had no monopoly on that curse....

Asa stood there, in the doorway of his two-room hovel, yellow oil-lamp light falling on his shoulders, with his woman's giving-birth hollers hammerin his brain, and looking out, past Alisha's horse, toward Panuke Road and its dark, wheel-rutted roadbed plunging and corkscrewing down the hillside toward the blacktop provincial highway. He could see, across the decrepit fields about, houses squatted in ruin, just a bright few looking habitable. He was thinking, there, in that blue-grey dusk, sharp tang of woodsmoke on the breeze, that this baby was a long time comin. Cynthy's second baby was takin some time. And it was gonna inherit, just like the first-born, what Asa'd inherited from a father who had only scraggly land, not even haggard love, to give. By golly, he could use some rum. But it was winter, Christmas only a couple days away, and not anything to chew on. Even weeds unobtainable now. Could there be any Pig Eating Good Cake, Scotch Cake with Scotch instead of brown sugar, rye coffee with some molasses, apples, pears, quinces, some sweet ham, roast chicken, dry herring, sausages with curry? Oh God, some roasted herring, strong ale, a bushel of cornmeal, anything that could go down good would be good. Christmas needs crackers, cheese, pound cakes, sweet potato pies, rice pudding, pumpkin pies, and mincemeat pies. But there ain' none. And no fat roast turkey, or real eggnog neither. Only the monotonously icy wind that was sheering off from the Atlantic, that desert of water, invisibly south over the gypsum hills, abandoning the dark, destructive icebergs where they lurked, and arriving as iced rain.

Asa was the fifth-generation Hamilton in Nova Scotia, and the third-generation to call Three Mile Plains home. But what a shack he'd gotten. He was now standing in the doorway where snow could come in anytime, the rain could blow out any little fire he could coax along. Unhygienic, it certainly be. The floor could flood with mud if there weren't enough newspaper tamped down, if the cracked, crooked window weren't blocked up somewhat with a plank, if the door had to groan open and off its hinges once too many times. In the front, a table, a few chairs, for gamblin, drinkin, smokin, whatnot. In the back, two beds, a dresser, and a washstand. Oil lamps took care of light, two small woodstoves hinted at heat. Yes, he complained about bedbugs and field mice. He had to take a shoe and kill the bugs on the walls, plus the field mice frozen scared on the sink or on the kitchen table. Everything smelled of coal dust and mouldering potatoes.

Not Asa. He smelled of the blood he brought from the butchery where he worked on and off. More off now. He was a meat cutter who thought he knew the Devil. He knew everything about animals brutally shredded. He had to clean up leftover animal bits, shovel away offal and shit and vomit, and kill cows himself, bash in their skulls, slash open their throats, to hurry on cessations. A Waterloo of hogs, a Somme of cattle. Awful noise and dirt. In a blood-soaked barn, thousands of pounds of meat hacked off of still-complaining animals in a crummy barn. Too often, blood and meat pieces slid inside his shoes, forming red, comfy extra socks. Him took this violence home with him, bundled up with meat scraps. And he was tired of ice-crusted piss in the chamber pot in the middle of a winter night, and he was tired of the memory of his widow mother having baby after baby by three or four jokers who liked fucking but didn't like fatherhood.

Asa's philosophy be belt straps and bullwhips on the ass; heftin sides of beef to feed corpulent palefaces; gulpin fast-fire tastes of wine outside a whites-only saloon; soiled food; Negress singers sirenin from a turntable, their raucous voices kickin the air. He could talk about worn-out shoes, worn-down blues, comment on scuffed-up record jackets. He didn't dream about porterin on the trains and goin on up to Montreal. Killin sheep paid better than shinin shoes and launderin sheets.

Now here was another bank-breaking, bottom-dollar Christmas. An unholy month of falling-down drunkenness. Nobody was gettin anything extra either. There was snow, there was rain, and it could go on like that for week after week; first, a downpour, then six feet of snow, as deep as the grave. The fresh snow collected in clumps, crannies, dark nooks. Then the winds come, heavier and heavier, unforgiving, heavy as hammers, unstoppable, refreshing, and sordid. Hard then to navigate a piece of land, a skirt of woods, a small stand of bush on the edge of Hants County, with so much sleeting mud, bone-chilling muck, then hazards of ice. Up over the hill and back a ways, Panuke Lake might wail bitterly with the cold. It could cry operatically as if a horse were stuck beneath its ice.

Asa winced to hear Cynthy holler a slobbering, sloping cry. Cripes! A foul season was winter, a shitty time for a baby to be shitted out, and here it was happening again, second year in a row.

Asa eyeballed a puddle near Alisha's horse. The water looked up idly at the sky like a mirror. Then the horse moved a hoof and broke the image. The sky was now muddled and quivering, promising drenching, punishing, and overflowing rains. But the horse's nostrils seemed caked with ice. Then Cynthy cried out sharply, and her second son slid into the world, on a flood of blood, in that two-room shack with dirty, tabloid-yellow floors.

The horse whinnied and Asa sighed. He'd better step back inside and swaddle the youngest. And how'd dour Alisha take her pay this time? Maybe the flesh bridge between baby and mother. Maybe she'd want that, to either eat it or bury it after chantin Afric-style over it. Asa walked back to the room where Cynthy lay crying, laughing, holding a copper-iron-coloured newborn in her arms, while Alisha, with the motions of a woman who saw no mysteries, moved a white rag over Cynthy's wet brow, and Cynthy looked up at Asa, who bent to see his new flesh.

She say, "After this one, no more, Asa. No more." And she laughed.

Asa muttered, "We already got one too many," and, quick as could be, Alisha slapped the fool man, and the newborn in his mother's arms wailed bitterly. Asa swore at Alisha to scram.

"Get fuck out ma house."

Alisha spoke, spookily, "If you don't hang God in your heart, Asa, you—or these boys—is gonna hang."

Asa spake: "You mumbo-jumbo bitch."

Cynthy warn, "Be kind, Asa." He glared.

Alisha spat, "I'm takin the cord to bury." Then she snapped up her things, snapped close her doctor's bag, and swept out.

Asa was alone with his family, and lonely. The sides of Cynthy's eyes glinted like aluminum in the pungent, smoky, weeping dark.

II

WHAT NEITHER Asa nor Cynthy knew was how much their personal destinies were rooted in ancestral history—troubles. Their own dreams and choices were the passed-down desolations of slavery. African Nova Scotia and, specifically, Three Mile Plains were the results of slave trade and slave escape. Three Mile Plains, Hants County, Nova Scotia, was, in fact, five, six miles of rolling hillsides directly southeast of Windsor town, which was forty-five miles northwest of Halifax, the provincial capital. The Negro—Coloured—people come from black slaves freed by redcoats down in Maryland and Virginia, then transported, like convicts, to "New Scarcity" during the War of 1812. They bore names like Johnson, Croxen, Grey, States, and Hamilton—the surname of John, a hellish master back on hellish St. Simon's Island in hellish Georgia. They arrived just like two thousand black others who came with nothing to nowhere, were landed with indifference and plunked on rocky, thorny land (soon laced with infants' skeletons), and told to grow potatoes and work for ale. They was so poor, they supposedly didn't even have history. And could they afford self-respect? Well, they paid for it with their backs, their legs and feet, their hands and arms.

The Plains people had since mixed with the Mi'kmaq, but only a few ancients knew exactly with whom and when. The results were splendid, though. These saltwater, brass-ankle

Negroes had bulbous noses, sharp black eyes, curly and partly straight hair, and skin tones running from deep molasses brown-black to maple sugar cream, auburn copper to red-iron, orange, and to blue. Their black hair could be blondish in places or high red. Also mixed up with whites, they often mirrored gorgeous Gypsies, possessing long black hair and copper skin, or even long blondish hair with cinnamon skin. They were nerve-rackingly, cinematically beautiful, terrifyingly, terrifyingly matinée-idol handsome. They looked like they stepped from a rainbow. Some trespassed onto fairgrounds and passed into carnivals as Moroccan showgirls or Indu dancers, and some posed as suspiciously English-only Cuban gangsters or became, easily, "New Yorkers" and went to Montreal where their shot-up corpses turned up in cars sunk into the Saint Lawrence River. Or they scrimped and saved and sent their children away to become professors of theology and umpteen languages, poets, and preachers, in Massachusetts, New Jersey, even New York City, North Carolina, Texas, and California. Or they became Commonwealth pugilists beating shit out of everybody—Yank, Caribbean, South American, African.

Three—Five—Mile Plains people had little plots of land to farm on long, sloping hillsides. They'd keep a few chickens, banty hens, cocks; a crude pen'd hold a prize pig; the prosperous could have a lettuce garden, apple trees, a cow, a horse. Other folks be pasted to scrawny fields of hay and tall grass and nothing else.

Originally, them stingy, shifty Brits had granted no one nough land to be an independent farmer. It was barbed-wire-fenced rocky, stony, pebbly field, very little red or black soil. Folks had to take hard rocks for pillows—and be happy. It were a starvation kingdom of consumption and cod. Hens clucked like whores. Dogs ate up the people's air and belched and bayed at their steps. Beyond the barren fields, there was pines, spruce, birch, alder, crabapple trees, oak, elm, maple, hazelnut bush, thorny raspberry canes, jetting blackberry canes, a Lombardy poplar or two, then train tracks and then the main road, Highway 1, yes, serpentine, and connecting the Annapolis Valley farmers (inheritors of land stolen from Acadians) with Halifax, southeast-bound.

But their local citadel was Windsor, or in Mi'kmaq, Piziquid. Situated at the marriage of the Avon and St. Croix rivers, it was a quarry full of "white gold"—"plaster of Paris"—gypsum. It were also business in limestone, wool, and apples. The town fronted on the Avon River, which, much muddier than the Bard's Avon, would flood and drain twice a day in rhythm with the "World's Highest Tides" in the Bay of Fundy. "Windsor-on-Avon" is acres of mudflats shimmering when the tide's bottomed out.

Plains Negroes had to go into Windsor to work. They went to the gypsum quarries, to the textile mill, the apple orchards, and into the mansions, all for pennies. In the gypsum pits, they saw buddies "axidentally" dynamited—arms, legs, flying through the air, or dropping dead of lung cave-ins, their breaths whitened by gypsum that blackened the guts. In the Windsor Clothiers factory, folks churned out thin cotton socks that disintegrated after one wear and one wash. Other Windsor Plains people made fiddles—and cash playin reels and jigs. There was work on the roads, driving a horse and cart. If a man got out of the quarry, he could milk cows (if he still had his hands). Privation was there in the boulders, in the starving hog, in the men mistakenly blasting each other into amputees for a wage of twenty-five cents a day, and calling themselves lucky. Some died broken, but everybody died broke. The people had to make their history with their sweat.

Many Plains' homes was ramshackle, lopsided boards, nailed together on crooked foundations, with no basement, only a hole for keeping potatoes. Rickets hit at tables; bureaus and sofas hobbled along on three real legs.

Still, in winter, as Asa knew too well, the tarpaper shacks with tin roofs was iceboxes, their cold embittering and chilling even embers. In such inclemency, folks could perish while cooking, or freeze into statuesque sleeping positions like Pompeii's fossilized figures. Or they had to humble and sip muddy water from pigpens.

The kerosene guy, Jack Clare, from the District of Clare, come only when the snow was deep. Folks heard the chop-chop of his horses' hooves over ice. Then they'd feel guilty and buy more than they needed. Then debt'd come on as mean as a gangster. Folks'd spend half the winter doubled up in pain from cutting ice for water or doubled up in fear of flu or bill collectors. When flu hit, people die faster than they can be buried. If it's Spanish flu, they die by the dozens and the half-dozens. There was tuberculosis set right in the snow, and cholera too. Or polio and rheumatism in how the rain fell. Or arthritis communicated by ice. Winter was no salt pork and brown biscuit to get anyone by. You got up in the dark, went to bed in the dark. You awoke with snow frosting your face because the window's like a gap between mountains. And no righteous eating, eh? If it wasn't possible to buy food, folks'd slaughter their horses, if they'd any. People would destroy the horses as they was eatin up the hay folks had to eat. Times they had to boil skinny, filthy rats for meat and take cholera water to drink. They was always between flu and whooping cough.

Joy was a beer. Food could be mud, drink just rain. Or it was potatoes and spring water, bread and molasses, cold chicken and beer. Holidays? Ill. Dominion Day was a big drunk, all day long. Everyone'd pass out, lie down, sprawling in roads, or stand up and piss against walls or squat and piss on floors. People plunked banjo and whistled harmonica along streams dragging through weedy fields, water gushing, plush, over weedy earth. It were a hillbilly Hell.

III

ONCE Alisha had gone off with the great prize of the navel string, Cynthy felt sad again. She mourned her once-loved fantasy that Asa was a gallant who was gonna spirit her out the narrow Valley, just spread his arms like Tarzan or Samson and push away all their troubles, and take her to fabulous Montreal, where style was brilliant, and where Coloured people could live posh—even if they had to speak French. Once, she'd even dreamt she was purring in a sixteen-cylinder Lincoln, a double-eight, a gigantic car that was like an aeroplane, and she and Asa were floating down Sainte-Catherine Street in Montreal, as big as life, waving at the jealous gawkers lining the sidewalks. When she smiled, in this delirious fantasy, her luxurious pleasure started at the back of her throat, if not deep in her lungs, then moved out to the surface of her face, rejuvenating and toning already youthful and graceful beauty muscles. The car stopped right at Eaton's, and she and Asa—who was wearing a black silk suit with a gold silk shirt, and she herself, in a dress deep-dyed a hymnal red—waltzed into the department store where, with the aid of curtsying mesdemoiselles, they selected racks of clothes to be put into barrels and sent down home. A voluptuous frisson had thrilled Cynthy's sleeping body, and when she awoke, she'd felt wet between her legs from what she imagined was a trickle of diamonds. Then she awakened and saw that the flow between her legs was the molten rubies of *Life* itself. But these material dreams had vanished in her monotonous universe of cabbage, cabbage, cabbage, cabbage, cabbage, and beans, beans, beans, beans, beans, beans, beans.

Three years back, when she'd said "I do," what she didn't know then, she knew now. Being Asa's lawful woman, he'd never let her abandon Three Mile Plains and its stony-hearted, stony-faced Negroes, and go on to Montreal, hear the Harlem bands, eat the smoked meat on rye sandwiches with a dill pickle slice, chant hypnotizing French, and spill champagne in champagne-coloured silk sheets. Problem was, it looked like Asa ain't got no drive; times too, he didn't even look good. He was clear muscle and hard bone, no fat on his frame: a square-headed, square-shouldered, black son of a bitch. He was so ugly, in actuality, Cynthy thought, that she could wear out a whole dictionary to describe just how sorry her husband was. What had been so beautiful now seemed disgusting. In their marriage she had gone from the molasses keg and its sulphurous sweetness to the pickle barrel and its salty sour. Instead of dying with laughter, out of joy, she felt like a laughingstock. She wanted to be petted, fondled, praised, kissed, licked, lapped, tickled, teased, spoiled, and made love to like in glamour magazines.

And she ain't forgotten, wouldn't ever forget, that red-suited white man at the Kentville train station, that same spring she'd met Asa, who whispered, suavely, "Now, as beautiful as Nova Scotia gals are, ain't ya the most beautiful brown Nova Scotia gal I ever see?" Why, he'd even pinched her patooty and praised her "plump and pleasant" rump.

"You're like a pretty little hurrah's nest, miss."

She were indignant to him, but the man guffawed, said, "You got talent to go with the type, I bet. I bet you could shimmy, tango, and warble blues to go."

Cynthy'd switched away from that red-silk-suited white man

with the blue tie, but he'd yelled at her sashaying bottom, "Ya come to Montreal, you come by Rufus's Paradise, he's a Negro gent who'll fix you up for big things."

Then the train puffed in and the red-white-blues man vamoosed. From then on, she'd craved Montreal. She even kept that name Rufus close to her heart. She knew she'd give it to a son for good luck. When her second son was born, she felt he was *spiritually* that white man's son. She'd have to go meet this Montreal Rufus.

What was Montreal? Her Harlem, her Heaven. From movie magazines and cousins, she knew it was rum that was fire in the mouth and satin in the belly. It was women who could cross ice—black ice—on stiletto heels and never fear losing their balance. It was women who could wear mink in the summer and make a hot day go chilly. It was being a show-offy dancer—a Chocolate Scandal—whose swishing bum would excite a man to dump his stash on drinks and tips. It was rye-and-ginger, Sweet Caporals, and smoky martinis. It was American cigarettes—caramel and tarty—and gangster *argot* and *panache*. It was elegant *café*-coloured legs and Ellington-like *café-au-lait* faces. It was a daily breakfast of brioches, croissants, orange juice, three cups of coffee, three beef sausages, an apple, and a muffin. Montreal was frontier Paris, a Habitant Manhattan.

Now there were two living babies amid the graveyard that Three Mile Plains could be, if they didn't get out. Cynthy called the new baby Rufus, or Rue. But he was a bother—rufous in tint and rueful in mood. Too much like his papa. Cynthy was headstrong though. She'd clear-cut a way.

She had to. It weren't possible for her to play a slave—Marie-Josèphe Angélique—or a saint—Joan of Arc—and exhibit such a painful degree of hurtful patience or of suicidal humility. Asa was too-goddamn insufferable.

Asa could raise his bull-faced fist and hit. He could whip her with a thin branch stripped to the green, hot sting. He could swear, "I'll hurt you in ways you'll wish to God you didn't have to be hurt." But Cynthy knew, on that dull morning in January 1927, she'd purchase a red dress, she'd go to Montreal.

So what if the Depression got in the way? For a woman without a cent to start with, money was just another luxury unnecessary for a "tolerable" life. Champagne could be rain and ginger ale; a ball gown could be cut from white women's cast-off curtains; cosmetics could be strained from berries and apples.

Cynthy's real tragedy was, her tyrannical household. She'd take a hotcomb to give her "good" hair more curl, and Asa'd snarl, "Why doncha just wear a do-rag?" The very looks that'd prompted him to give her two boys, now just seemed to aggravate his impoverishment: "Inky bitch gotta have kinky hair." Or with a mouth that spat pure vinegar, he damned her as a hard-bitten bitch, a narrow, un-manning bitch. His honest emotion was sweat. Her marriage was an orchard of rotten fruit and dry, snapped branches, a wormy atmosphere. Not to mention cold winds, chilly rooms, cold gruel, and a bed frozen in frigidity.

Asa was no longer crazy for incuntation with her. After a gallon of plonk, he'd go stumbling, jaundice-eyed, tar-faced, cussing, up and down the road, seeking some thoroughbred hussy, with his foul lust sticking out, dripping, his cock looking like dried-up muck, a worm of snot dangling from a nostril, and his whole being reeking of pork-scented smoke. And what he squandered outside their doors, on booze and big-ass broads, Cynthy couldn't question. She couldn't say to him, "Come with the truth, or leave your dog-ass home," cos he'd slap her down, leave bloody spittle on her lips, put her out her own house. Times she was tempted to slink down dusty, pot-holed Panuke Road, to lay her burdens down by laying her head on the train tracks, or to hold her two boys in her arms like two

loaves of bread and stand in front of a smoking locomotive
stampeding to Halifax. But she needed to survive—to revive
soulfully in Montreal.

Faced with Asa's fists, his cussing tongue, and his lack of
even a pittance of respect for her—a woman whose skin should
smell of Moir's fine chocolates, whose beautiful hair should
always boast gold ribbons, and whose wardrobe should bristle
with furs and shimmer with silks, Cynthy began to hope Asa
would just drink rum and die. Or perhaps another man, hungry
for her favours and angry at Asa's shameless, fitful, alcoholic
pawings of her excellence, would stick a shotgun at the back of
Asa's skull and pull the trigger. His horror, his ludicrous
rummy's stagger, his skin transporting the stench of greasy,
sallow big fat bitches, all had to perish so Cynthy could be a
beauty who could sit in windows and be admired. In a red dress.

Why'd she need to fuss with some fool whose brain was
muddy with rum? She desired fried liver with fried onions,
fried chicken with rum, or fish 'n' chips with salt and vinegar.
Not constant pork—ham hocks, pigtails, sausages, tripe from
the butchery. How could her looks be sustained
by pigs?

A nightmare of a dream, Asa made their lives a rum-splashed
Damnation; he was Satan to Cynthy and their sons. The belt
touched them so much, it was like their best suit of clothes. The
wanton rage inside him was a lake of fire and melting rocks, as
volcanic as alcohol, his one true faith. All they saw was a daddy
who, after a nasty slug of rum, would "paint" the outhouse toilet with the dirt of his mouth or his ass.

Polluted by their papa's mean drunkenness, the boys grew
like poisonous weeds. They were already learning to slip their
skinny fists into that drunkard's pockets to find any bit of
coin they could—even if they got smacked or punched for
their troubles. They spent their thefts on candy, bubblegum,

potato chips, soda pop. Cynthy almost regretted letting her boys be born, for they were the phantoms of a devil father: they seemed like two good-for-nothings already, with their household thieving and angry lying, and they'd not even gone to school yet.

Throughout her sons' infancy and her husband's rummy vileness, Cynthy came more and more to fancy a red dress as an emblem of civilization, one higher than that she knew. For four years then, every time Asa came in drunk, and she could get to clean his pockets before her sons did, she'd take the cash and coins and hide them away. She hoarded secretly what she managed to finagle, finesse, and filch from that monster of a husband. For four years, every time Asa cussed, slapped, or whipped her, she found a way to put away money.

It was possible to live without money, for that's what Cynthy had to do. But money was still a salve. Money was good for— one day—herring fillets, kippers, unwatered-down wine, a red dress, and a ticket to Montreal. Money was for bucking beds that couldn't break. Money was for skin smooth as licorice, for hair as straight as licorice, for breath as sweet as licorice, and for eyes as dark as licorice. Above all, money was for a scarlet-crimson-red dress that could be set off by a white scarf. And didn't she admire redwood, red chile, red cinnamon, and red wine? The best way to ward off Asa's evils was, Cynthy believed, to indulge in a dress whose red was opulent and perfect for a carmine-lipped woman with apple-smooth skin.

It was January 1931 when, passing through Windsor town in the wake of the Xmas Shopping Sales, she saw a sumptuous dress in the windows of the shop owned by Flora Carat. The dress shone with an April-like brilliance even in the dead-end of winter. In that red dress, Cynthy imagined she could set all Three Mile Plains ablaze with crimson, see the landscape blazed in scarlet. Just flowers, flowers, flowers. She'd afford tantrums of red, a religion of red.

She went into the bedroom and got the sixteen dollars she'd pinched and wadded and hidden in a tin can inside a hole in the floor under the crib. She forgot her boys now. Jangling gently because of the change bulging her purse, she tramped through snow, flagged down an eye-roving man who saw just her juicy, lightly clad bottom (she was only wearing her nightgown under her thin black wool coat), and got into Windsor, went to Madame Carat's Paris Dress Shop, looked into Carat's green Siamese-cat eyes, plunked down the coins, and bought a red crushed-velvet dress. Cynthy made sure that Madame Carat tied up the box real pretty, with a red ribbon and a bow. (She could later use the ribbon in her hair.)

When she left Madame Carat's shop, Cynthy didn't just walk through snow; now, she marched through it, militantly proud, her head sky-high. She felt deliciously rich—a Cleopatra of the pines—and though she'd not have the shoes to match the dress, though the dress itself would be conspicuous in her closet, like a rose jutting from sawdust, though other women would loathe her for her *expensive* look, Cynthy was delighted. She felt so good, she couldn't feel the wind drilling into her body like a host of circus knifethrowers' blades, nor the snow that snuck down chillingly into her ankle-high boots with almost every other step.

When Cynthy arrived back at the shack, its guts spooked by the oil lamp's malevolent shadows, Asa had already discovered the open hole in the floor beneath their bed and had decided what it meant. She knew when she saw his slit-eyed look at her coming through the door, while she brushed snow from her shivering shoulders and held that inexplicable box crooked self-consciously under one arm, that a cave-man rage would seize him like an epileptic fit. George and Rufus ran out to meet her, expecting the box to contain gifts for them. But Asa barked at them to get to their beds. They shrank back into their shadows. Cynthy steeled herself against Asa's leaden anger.

Before Cynthy could say a word, Asa's fist slammed her face like a rum bottle; the precious box flew from her grip; she fell.

"That cash—you sly, yella bitch—was Easter!"

She laughed, blood jerking from her nose: "Dumb-ass nigger!" Her venom was her champagne—in that hut where perfume itself seemed derisory. While his infants wailed, Asa uncoiled his belt from his pants, made a loop of that leather, then straddled his fallen, bleeding wife and treated her like he was tenderizing horse meat. Then he tore the clothes right off Cynthy's squirming, writhing body and raped her, screeching, on the blood-muddied floor. George and Rufus wailed, watched. Their pa's curses lashed out like a pimp's coat hanger wire—slick, hot, whipping. Then he burnt Cynthy's brand-new red dress in the woodstove's red fire. Cynthy imagined hammerin a spike through Asa's bony and backward heart. Such a brittle target should splinter like dry chicken bones, releasing marrow like dust.

IV

GEORGE and Rufus was born in two grim, cold, influenza Decembers, no need for Christmas, in a shack that couldn't even play a manger. No pig would've been happy to bed down in the squalor to which the two black boys was introduced. Their childhood was cups of grease on a battered table; rat poison set out carefully, carefully, like meals fit for kings; hailstorms wiping out any pretty good crop; lovely, heavy crops reduced to blotches by too much water; a horde of hail and a flood of rain carrying off everything. At a young age, they watered down ketchup to make juice. This was poverty, East Coast–style, and it had a long pedigree. It was an apocalyptic genealogy. That was the household defined: lots of knives but hardly any real meat, fish, cheese, or real food. One compensation: Asa could take guts, tripe, stuff picked up from the knackery floor, get a bagful, bleeding, carry it home.

But Asa had to root out stubbornness—in both dame and pups. His own family was, he felt, treacherous. He hid money from Cynthy, just in case she decided whimsically to go to Montreal, or to spend every cent on another triflin dress. Asa knew she was still desirous of Montreal, and George and Rue was always glancing defiant at him.

One day when the boys were six and seven, the knackery'd paid Asa twenty dollars in cash, all in ones, and he'd come whistling home with a piggybank-fat wallet. He felt smart, fit, and wanted. He was—temporarily—a rich man during a cease-less Depression. Seething with joy, he walked up Panuke Road as the sun abandoned the sky and the fields full of August corn. Feeling warm-hearted, soon as Asa come in the door of his shack, he opened his wallet and spilled twenty smackeroos on the table. He looked at Cynthy, who looked back with a tight smile. Next thing he knew, she'd snatched up five dollars, while the boys scooted back and forth, caterwaulin and hollerin, "Candy! Candy! Daddy, buy us candy!" The din was irksome, but Asa felt most cross with his wife. The sun lanced a final blade of light through the waxpaper-thin curtain on the kitchen window as Asa said, without menace, "Gimme it back."

Cynthy said, "The boys need new clothes."

Blood swelled up Asa's veins in his head and throat. "You don't care bout clothes! All you care about is you! So help me. Nah, ya ain't gettin nothin." George and Rufus stopped play-ing; they began to edge, scared, toward the bedroom. The air in the shack singed them like dry fire. Asa shot them incinerating looks. Cynthy ordered them to bed. Then she stuck her five rolled-up bills in her bra.

Asa said, "Ain't tellin ya again." Cynthy levelled shotgun-deadly eyes at him. Asa stepped up to the side of the stove and picked up a healthy hickory stick. Cynthy said again she needed the money for Rue and George.

Asa growled. "Ya gonna defy me?"

Asa meant to show "gumption." He lit into Cynthy. He lathered her so hard that the woman's body.... The switch sunk blisters wherever it hit, then it'd crack em open. Blood hissed on—and under—her mistreated skin. Asa galled her bony, bent-over, black back. The stick split her spine into welts and stripes. Its crack mimicked the cracking of glass, of bone, a heart.

George and Rufus scurried out to try to help their mother. But Asa was sore enraged. He cut up his boys too. They crawled under the kitchen table to escape; Asa seized slow ankles and hauled em out. He'd cut em good on their nakedness, like an overseer striking a slave. The brothers squatted, squealed like rats, but the switch still come down, come down—*Kermash!*—and it was lash, blood, screams, tears, cries, lash, blood, screams, tears, cries. The branch came down, down—*Smash!* Asa lathered his sons to straighten out, he felt, their cut-eye, double-talking, loud-mouth, suck-teeth behaviour. They had to learn they were worth zilch. He was a patriarch who felt commissioned to destroy his family. His fist had to smash the air, smash the rum bottle down on the scarred table, smash the table down, smash the wife down onto her fuckin knees, smash the boys into two corners of the scuttling shack. The boys had to be abused like beasts, just whipped and slapped and kicked and punched and beaten, so they'd knuckle under and be quiet niggers.

Asa say, "Ya ain't big enough to beat me yet. When ya's big enough, ya try an beat me." These children—his very own— was gonna be niggers, not engineers. So the boys heard their father's stick baying at them; they heard it strike and strike and strike. Oh God, oh God, oh God. They had to piss and shit themselves—just like their mother. Their blood had to smirk from the end of his stick. Flesh Mama made, Pops unmade. His switch was an incisor biting down from mouthy air to gnash and gnaw on two boys and a wife like joints of raw meat.

By the time Asa stopped walloping his family and had ripped those five one-dollar bills from Cynthy's bra, he was sobbing sweat and his wife and boys were weeping blood. Too, the bills was so sodden and stained, the King's face thereon so ruined, Asa knew he'd have to explain to businesses taking them that he'd meant no defiling of the sovereign.

Against this backdrop of stupidity and calamity, the boys was put to mind the chickens, bony, to tend the pigs, scrawny. Also, Georgie'd have to fill the coal lamps every morning, first, he'd wipe the soot off glass chimneys lest they break. Nights, he'd darken the light. George also milked neighbours' cows and helped collect cream. He'd take cream, let it sour, then pour it into a churn. He'd plunge the dasher up and down to foam up sugary butter. Then he'd spoon the cream—good-quality sweet scum—right off the milk, clean and salt it, and wrap it in wax paper to sell for so many cents a pound. Here was happiness.

Times, the brothers'd skin hides, or go out to collect junked bottles. May to August was the toiling months. They'd paper the outhouse with pictures from the Eaton's catalogue; use those same pictures to clean themselves. They'd coat mules and horses with oil and pine tar to frustrate mosquitoes. (They wore it too.) They'd go foresting and slingshot squirrels, then slice off and hang the skins on coat hangers to dry. In winter, they eyed horses bringing fresh vegetables; they eyed horses carting away fresh coffins. They froze fish to gnaw on in the spring. They hefted boxes of coal now and then. They gave Cynthy every nickle they made, till they got to smoking.

But the boys didn't work well together. Rufus hated farm work and George just wanted to eat. The worst time was when a pig tumbled down the well and just floated there: Asa made the boys hoist it out and kill it—just to teach it a lesson. Rufus had to hammer in the animal's squealing face because Georgie couldn't handle knives. Rue pounded in the animal's skull while George squatted and threw up his yellow guts into the green grass and the pink pig squealed, moaned, squirted blood, shit.

To school, the guys went barefoot, at least in late spring and early fall. In fall and winter, they pulled on double pairs of socks and moccasins. Do that, or wrap their feet in gunny sack, so they wouldn't freeze and needs be "decapitated." In the school, a newspaper portrait, a painting in colour of George V, shared the front wall with a crayon rendering of Christ and a tacked-up tattered Union Jack. These pictures smiled on the few white kids and damned most of the black ones: that's how the boys felt. And forget about having anything to themselves at their school: no books, no pen, no ink, no pencil, no paper smelling like mackerel. No tubby bottle of LePage's glue, no piles of Hilroy scribblers, no heaps of Eberhard-Faber pencils, no red-leather-bound old books—yellowed bits of history— and no bottles of squid-black, Parker ink. They'd have to sit and memorize the lessons, or try to share the paper and pencils of other pupils. Everyone plunked on long pine-plank benches. (Heat in winter came from the cast-iron potbelly woodstove.) They were careful not to anger Miss Jarvis, lest she stick a three-inch-long fingernail in their ears.

Miss Jarvis once told Rue, "You got the light of God in your face."

Rue parried, "No, ma'am, that's just the lamplight."

A visiting white teacher called Rufus "a sly little nigger boy." Big for his age, he slapped her. He got strapped in school, then whipped at home. That was Grade Three, when he was ten, and so he quit.

For Georgie, too, school composed a boxing ring. White kids would throw chalk dust in his face "to make ya white," and he'd scrap, his brown fists flailing like those of George Dixon—Kid Chocolate—that sharp, Halifax middleweight. He'd tap a chum with his fist, see if his target'd crumple. But he was a bruiser, quick, unthinking: truly Asa's son. Times, Rue'd help, and dab a guy in the jaw, watch him fall like an axed tree. But Rue could only throw so many punches on George's behalf. So Georgie fell out of school too, aged eleven in Grade Three.

The boys picked up most of their letters by digging into comic books and sitting, hypnotized by silvery wisps on hallucinatory screens, in movie theatres. They scrounged grammar—a rough version—from radio gangster shows.

The boys looked Cuban; they looked Mexican; they looked Gypsy; they looked Indian; they looked Injun. To themselves, they looked decidedly, properly handsome. To others, they looked like trouble. But what they were looking for was love—and respect.

V

ASA'D ALWAYS had an eye for playing cards picturing topless blondes and brunettes. He felt Coloureds was slag heaps of men wanting diamonds of (white) women. Talkin with gypsum quarry Coloureds, he knew about a special house in Windsor town, a subtle palace run by Gabby Robie, the local sports reporter. There, no one cared if a raven and a dove commingled. There, liquor was being sold, gals was being sold, hog was being sold. So when he waxed violently tired of Cynthy, her Montreal mania and her cash complaints, Asa rented hisself a creamy tart.

When Asa found, in the backside of Windsor, the right oak back door, knocked, and was admitted, his moviehouse-dim eyes scoped Purity Mercier, gleaming through the lamplight and cigar and cigarette fog. She be to him a lithe brunette with a snow complexion. White bones basked in her arms, her sleek gams, her *terra alba* skin, the silky feel of an anglicized *Acadienne*. Her perfume was the smell of sunlight and rain and the moment that rain evaporates. Asa wasted no time wasting half his pay that Friday night on Purity. Joined with her, he experienced a vaudeville show of whinnying, oinking, snorting, gasping, spitting, and drooling, fore and aft.

The every-Friday-night Asa–Purity duo was an importation of Othello-and-Desdemona Venice to Windsor-on-the-Avon. He wished he could fuck till the stable were shaking, shaking, and falling down around them, moistly. Purity was weekend payback for each weekday of lonely hate. True: Asa liked the look of her lily hands dabbling in, dallying with, the hot coal of black male flesh.

Asa became a regular fool, much to grubby, rancid Gabby's enrichment. Purity was one more victim, a woman from the impoverished, French-speaking countryside that couldn't speak French and prosper. Like many Acadians, she'd been Englished in merciless schools and Anglicanized by predatorial bosses. These Anglo-Saxons had palms always moist for the hot love of coin; and eyes always hot with lust for their female workers. Purity felt a bit more freedom and realized a bit more cash enduring the degradations of Gabby's bordello than she did in suffering the depredations of heartless factorists.

In response to Purity's needling spontaneity, a kerosene-hot lust'd snake up Asa's thighs, into his pelvis, then all up along his backbone, and into his skull. She always seemed as impatient as a breaker and twice as wet. There was indigo doings inside ivory toings and froings. Joyous chaos of white legs akimbo where Asa's were a randy Sambo's. Red wine wrinkling throats and puckering lips.

Asa'd mumble his hallelujah, and then he was zippered up, liquored up, and gone out Purity's door, exited her deal-wood kennel, blundering through smoke or fog, then staggering across grass sparkling late night with, at times, dew-reflected stars, and then along the roadway, stopping to piss in ditches, or pass out there, until stumbling back to Three Mile Plains, only five miles away, to plunge to the depths a bottle of rum could reach. He was bleakly happy, but still dissatisfied. Asa's brain spewed crazy phrases.

"Another slurp, please....Skedaddle from one gulp to the next.... I feel the wall coming upside my head.... My stomach is shit.... I don't want dribs and drabs; I want the gush.... I'll crouch, take a sip, fall over...."

He sing "Black Flowers":

> *Lookin for a face that won't quit my eyes.*
> *Lookin for her face that'll suit my eyes.*
> *Lookin for her thighs to—tight—fit mine.*

Asa'd whip Cynthy if she complained about the cash he fed Gabby. He'd clip her upside the head, slam her across the spine, belt her if she gave any lip. It was his bloody money, his funky flesh, his sweaty business.

Cynthy detested her jointly adulterated marriage—which was really a slow-motion divorce, but with no property to divide. She fantasized more and more about mixing rat poison into oatmeal served with milk and honey, or of picking up kerosene oil and confusing it with vinegar. A smartly paced poisoning of Asa Hamilton could liberate her—Cynthy Croxen (she'd recover her maiden name)—more sweetly than any set of prayers. But she was no chemist, and doctors and police might discover her petty treason, and, though not unhappy that another quarrelsome dark man was dead, still send her to jail for way too long.

Too, her sons were uninteresting to her now, save for Rufus, who always gave evidence of shifty thinking. But Georgie was as dull as Asa. Rufus was real slick. She felt seduced by him. But George be oafish, but useful. Rue reminded her sweetly of what that white man had said to her, when she was sixteen, in the train station. Times, Cynthy remembered to play mother. When Georgie was twelve, she sewed him a quilt got from twenty-pound sacks of Five Roses flour. She was goodness itself—when she could convince herself to be maternal.

Nevertheless, Cynthy, unable to get to Montreal and unable to keep Asa at home, took lovers of her own, but discreetly, so as not to unleash Asa's fists. She was sick of facing dirt instead of glamour. She started dragging her bony ass all up and down Panuke Road and into backwoods too, whenever Asa had his back turned. She wanted revenge for that burnt-up red dress. She lay the rusty must of her sex all over several Hants County shacks. She had to sweat and groan like some infernal engine, a piston plunging therein. Her flower-flesh, once the colour of the apricot nectar rose, her petally fragrance, both surrendered to dirt and stink. This thin, hickory-smoked woman, her hair smelling of homemade pomade got of real *pommes*—a randy, McIntosh scent, had hair straighter than her soul now was. She experienced a failure of discrimination. Some men she laid with were often so drunk on rum that Cynthy would get drunk just off their breaths and sweat. But so what? Sex was like aspirin; it was like eating sugar, sugar, sugar; it was income with an outgoing attitude.

Cynthy soon selected Reverend Simon Dixon as her chief man. He was skilled at the subtle fucking of wives. Yep, he loved hogs, whores, and wine, in no apparent order, and adultery was his prized sin because he was single and had steady money.

He say, "I's from the Society for the Propagation of the Species." He loved carrying on with wives all Saturday who sat, prim and proper, beside husbands in church on Sunday. He could preach so hotly about Hell, he'd gush sweat from every pore while some very upright ladies—Hell-deserving, Sunday-praying Jezebels—would piss their drawers. No, he had no use for the Bible he kept nostalgically, its pages scribbled over with gibberish, its pages all blotted and blotched and yellowed and taped together, its spineless self. Whenever he parted holy text, he departed from that text. He was one of those ministers, not just fallen, but always *falling, in flagrante delicto*, as lithe and proud as a saint, into down beds. He was a scurrilous pastor staggering through hilly plains and preaching the ugliness of Christ, the bitterness of Christ, the loneliness of Christ. His entry into Cynthy's bed marked her epochal drift away from her sons. Dixon was a promise of a red dress and a train ticket to Montreal.

So, with Georgie gone twelve and Rue eleven, Cynthy up and dumped her sons in Alisha's backyard, right in December 1937, a hungered season, and just turned her back. The winter was already bruisingly bitter. That ice-daggered wind slashing into Cynthy's face while she dragged squalling Georgie and sullen Rue onto the yard of Alisha's rough and uncouth house, painted charcoal black, with her ghost-callin bottles hung on the branches; a dog slobbering, pissing like a horse, and yowling blackly and pulling at the heavy chain that held it back; and Alisha's horse tethered weirdly to a railroad track switch plunked down ex-nowhere. The top half of a horse's skeleton sat at the wheel of a rusted-out convertible. Then, Alisha was eyeing Cynthy approach her house, her kitchen curtain pulled back with one strong thin black hand. But Alisha didn't come welcome em: this bad idea was foretold. Huffing, cussing, even cuffing the bawling George, the cut-eye Rue, Cynthy finally got em to Alisha's house, then pounded on the door with a gloved hand, before racing back to the road where sly Reverend Dixon waited—his cream car and engine purring, his jaundiced, gooey look congealing—to schmooze Cynthy to Halifax, epic city of concubinage.

VI

RUE shed no tears at Cynthy's vanishing. He already understood that "I love you" equals two parents and a bastard: *I, you,* and *love*. Jawgee and Rufus was just black boys blackened further by Depression. They were two pieces of shit that Cynthy just had to put somewhere. The falling snow hammered a prison into shape around them. Snow belted them like their father's hand.

Alisha cared for the brothers for a month: she showed them all the hidden things in her house so that they could see she had no bank of jewellery or coin. In fact, Alisha had no cash: she lived by barter, prayers traded for firewood, a medical cure exchanged for a side of beef. Still, she showed the boys—who she knew were already thieves—she had nothing worth stealing.

George and Rue were glad to stay with Alisha because they ate better with her. Bean soup and corn cake and "smothered" rabbit stew and liver (free off the meat truck) and heart and kidneys (also free), plus roast beef, corn beef, salt fish (delivered in barrels off trucks), tons of sauerkraut, salt pork, root vegetables, too.

When Cynthy reappeared from Halifax and from that affair that had netted her only a new coat, she took the boys back like nothing. Asa hit her of course, but she felt no pain because her hatred was like that of a martyr. While the sun cringed amid the kitchen's kerosene and cranky smoke, Asa's assault was like an ascension for her.

Cynthy waited one April morning till Rue and Asa had gone out, then she called George over to her bed and sat up with only her black filmy negligée on, so he could eye her sumptuous breasts and she could enjoy his confusion, and she seized his arms, then his head, and clasped him infant-close, maternally, to her breasts, and asked him for a favour.

He gulped, said, "Okay, Mama." She reached under the bed and pulled out two bottles of rum.

She said, "Don't tell your no-good pappy on me. I need yer help, Joygee. Just take these bottles to the school and sell each one for two dollars—nothin less. Okay?" She also nagged him to bootleg cigarettes to his school chums. George nodded, carried the bottles and smokes to school, but he felt intimidated by the big boys, them aged sixteen in Grade Four. He was properly afraid they'd just smack im and grab the rum and cigs. He begged Rue to help with the sales. Rue was a natural, and prospered at this trade. He was convinced Georgie was just a slobbering crybaby.

Georgie didn't like doing what his Mama said he must do: bootleg. But Rue didn't like what Cynthy and Asa was doing— taking food out their mouths to go out fucking with. Everybody had to put up or shut up. Rue found means to make his way.

At twelve, and big for his age, Rufus took a bus into Windsor on a Saturday to see a show, but stopped by the grocery store. A cute boy, he'd learned how to be a charmer, and, at the grocery store, had so honeyed and sweet-talked the white cashiers, they cooed, blushed, and give him candy. But he had other plans. As soon as they were busy with customers, he slipped back into the coatroom and emptied their purses and coatpockets. He got fifty dollars, smooth, easy, and clear. And he didn't get caught. When he got home, he went straight to the moonlit woods and dug beside a crabapple tree to hide a tin can full of money. The next day, he took Georgie back into the woods to show him his stash and swore him to silence. Georgie kept the secret, but he also kept half the cash by threatening to tell Asa what Rue had done. From then on, Rufus fingered Georgie for a traitor.

What could he do to survive an incandescently ugly papa, an operatically sluttish mama? Chewing tar was good for whitening teeth, but was no real entertainment; smoking cast-off cigarette butts was entertainment, but no profit; a lengthy mouthful of bootleg could be a profit, but not yet a business. Still trying to discover a life, a way to make himself a living, he reconnoitred an old, abandoned house containing see-sawing planking for floors, a cleaver of sunlight chopping through a chink in the kitchen walls, an antique, mouldering piano in a light-drenched parlour, and obliquely black shadows hounding the piano keys. There he could consider coltish, skittish, cinnamon-and-chocolate sirens in silk and cashmere, their sweat like satin, their moans like wine, their skin, either euphoric gold or dark, very dark, carbon black, without any painful whiteness.

This old house belonged to a minister who'd died and whose daughters spurned Three Mile Plains. They locked it up after the casket came out with their father inside, and they just rode off with their husbands. Then the lock rusted off, "pickanninies" smashed out the windows with rocks, ragpickers carted off everything portable, then the rain and snow came in, the foundation buckled, the house slumped like a dead whale. Now Rue, aged thirteen, had clambered into the fallen-down house, cross its crazy, tilting, madly squawking floors, examine the yellowed and bleached sepia pictures on the walls, glance at the shattered china scattered every which way, piss in the cobweb-mapped bathroom (inhale its smell of antique must, its aroma of old rugs and mildew), navigate floors with grass leaping through and snakes sliding through holes like open sores, look out windows now splintered reflections on the floors, and then sit at the rotting grand piano, still bearing leaves of faded sheet music. This instrument, even with the trunk of a pear tree coming up through one side of its body so that only some keys could be played, even with its seeming drift toward a sinkhole in the parlour floor, was still a fountain of notes, discordant, compelling. The piano was elegant ebony, a being once pulled to the door of the Reverend Ohio States's home by ox-team. Music became Rue's consolation. While Asa turned to booze, Rue turned to art.

He had no training, but he had temper. Alone, he'd bash those playable keys; alone, he'd admire the gorgeous congress of Negro and Caucasian keys, so capable of beautiful intimacy here, but not in Three Mile Plains, not in Nova Scotia. In the rest of the world too, such couplings were secret and brutal. The unheard-of melodies—strange—that Rufus hammered out on that piano were the Nova Scotian discovery of jazz and blues, if anyone had heard and said "Amen." Bothered by inexplicable longings that cut through his bowels like hot water, he tried to follow memories of radio tunes that came out of black women's redemptive mouths. He'd heard Bessie Smith—big, brown, brassy Bessie and all her blues about oversexed coffee grinders and jelly rolls and generators. He loved that voice—its symphony of proverbs—all the more. What Bessie sang was immaculately filthy. There was a wah-wah wail he had to have, a piano rag that came from scrutinizing Disney cartoons in the moviehouse in Windsor. The piano became his confessional, his brothel, his hospital, his church, his army, his canteen, his library, and his school. It was refuge from a lust-busted-open shack on Panuke Road. Rue loved to feel and hear his fingers striking handsomely against a half-playable keyboard, with no knowledge of mistake or failure or trespassing or vandalism. He transmitted, without knowing it, all the lovely Negro poetry of the United States. He hammered out his broken-hearted genealogy in each phrase torn from the rotting heart of half a piano. Too, Bessie sang on, her voice black with pain—or black with a writhing, sweaty pleasure.

In the midst of his music and this homely space, Rue felt peace. He could defecate on the ground and use leaves to cleanse himself, then wipe his hands off on the dewed grass; he could smash and ruin intrusive household insects; he could dream of Ellington piano; Ellington jackets—natty, velvet; and Ellington nights with fresh girls—spicy, smoky—one of each type balanced, naked and preening, on each knee.

Rue coaxed from half a keyboard hour after hour of braying, bellowing, cawing, squawking, and grunting notes. His was a Negro language of ripping, cutting, smashing, and destroying sounds—the sounds of the slaughterhouse and the sounds of the whorehouse.

Sometimes he'd just lounge in that music-haunted abode and leaf through comic books. A panel'd show a razor gashing a long hole in a face; another would show a gangster plugging a body falling like a thrown-down overcoat; or a white moll, blonde, would be pushed off a skyscraper and end up smashing in the roof of a black late-model car. His eyes roved over pages of cartoon women's pinkish, "flesh"-coloured faces and bullet-shaped breasts; but also women who were light casketed in dark lanterns, women as golden as gold trumpets of dark rum.

Rue painted these images in the music he drew from that half-dead keyboard, its keys going *thud, thud.* And the instrument kept sinking further into the caving-in floor. The keyboard warped more and more starkly, what with all the rain rinsing and gurgling into that splayed house. Stars cracked through the roof and ceiling, the floors turned to dirt; the piano was clouded and choked by pear-tree petals. The piano got carried off by the rampant pear tree. One more failure for Rue.

Irritated by the collapse of the keyboard, its branching off into the rigging of a tree, its refusal of music in favour of nectar,

Rue, still desiring sound, still lusting to employ professionally dextrous fingers, exchanged music lessons for pistol ones. He bought a stolen .32, shiny as a crucifix, and wasted all his bullets by firing at the placid heads of sunflowers. To be dapper like Pretty Boy Floyd. He go out into a neighbour's sunflower grove. He hated those lustful-looking sunflowers tossing their yellow faces lasciviously. He fired wantonly. Those sunflowers had their heads exploded. No one found out who wrecked so disgustingly sixteen sunflowers. What was left of em charred black, in winter, in the once-pure-yellow fields. Rue buried the pistol; it was no good without bullets. His discharging over.

While Rue had been in the music field, sort of, Georgie was in the cornfield. Rue beat on a banged-up piano; Georgie beat on two broken-down mules. Out of school now three years, and aged fourteen, of the two brothers, he was truly the "country" one: even his name was royally agrarian. His holidays was in the fields.

Georgie got work in Windsor for twenty-five cents a day, plus board, way back in the lumberwoods, and doing odd jobs. He was always grubbing trees, toting away rocks, planting crops, and pulling up weed roots. An honest living. He chopped land. Tending gardens, he savoured the ones featuring fruit trees, plums, gooseberries, currants, or strawberries, maybe even some awesome onions and gigantic watermelons (unlike the itty-bitty ones Cynthy planted).

His dungarees smelled of tobacco smoke. He knew that no rabbit's foot was truly lucky unless it'd first been dipped in alcohol. (A snagged rabbit could bring in fifteen cents.) He knew how to whistle, but knew no jazz. He loved April for its water, fresh and sweet and pure and cold water. Each April, rain drooled through the new maple leaves after hurricanes of lightning—with considerable thunder and truly striking light. Then came rattling brooks, garrulous. He'd watch scraggly apple trees struggle into blossom. He enjoyed the odd tinkle of rain because each drop was noisy ointment for flowers. (Rain is how the sea summers in grass.) But he also saw how too-heavy rain could fire the brown earth to grey. The crabapple tree in the yard would blossom whitely and ironically sweet: its fruit would be sea-green with sourness. The fields about Three Mile Plains and Hants County flowered pure clover and strawberries. Apples, blackberries, and raspberries could be gobbled down along the railway tracks. In the backwoods, the maple leaves used to tickle and harass him, lewdly. Crows'd ring his head—like a bizarre halo—when he'd go out. He watched black horses riot out of fog. He spied smelts running in the creek and blueberries sunning in the fields. He'd streak through fields just like a mouse, enjoying his own sleek scurrying, the rush of tall grass against his shins, his thighs, his chest. He could walk straight as a bullet. He could swill rain and gobble berries. He'd get up in the dark, come home in the dark. His muscles waxing as the daylight waned.

Power was in George's arms and legs: he could swing a big axe like a little hammer. He used a seven-pound axe back in the woods. He'd hack down maples and hack up ash. He'd hack up rampikes into logs and logs into kindling like none of your business. He'd hove to and fro until each pine or maple was a goner. The work was tough; his muscles got to be damned enormous. His hands were bad-ass carpenters, ingenious mechanics. He got some cash for cutting logs, using a cross-saw and an axe. He hauled hard against horses but looked just like a bull. He hewed timber by the Annapolis River. (He poured his axe into the tender, virgin flesh of pines. They quivered every time he stroke.) He looked stocking-capped and singing, his adolescent moustache all flecked with woodchips and sawdust. His saw was a healthy steel that sang. He'd bustle into the fields, get the bulls hitched.

He sweated with Percherons, huge workhorses weighing a half a ton each.

October staged funerals of ripe fruit and vegetables in autumnal cauldrons. Maples, oaks, aspens, birches, coldly ablaze. Windfall apples sprawled frosty some mornings. Frost heaving everything up. Crackling, superficial ice defined November. George'd work well into the cold days, then work even better into warmed-up rum. He liked to trek through daytime, rainy snow—snow as cold or as warm as rain—cross barrens made palatable by blueberries, stick-and-stone together a small, smoking fire, then boil tea, bake a potato, fry apple slices, stew venison or cook a duck. To abracadabra autumn back into April.

Game'd keep well from October to April. George'd let deer meat break down to get the rigor mortis out, to get it so tender he could cut it with a simple knife. Such know-how could turn moose and deer into snowshoes and moccasins; hunger could turn them into mincemeat. George sawed ice that was thick, cutting out squares like cakes already frosted. He could get hungry, starving, dreaming the ice was cake.

Georgie's first love was food. Life was a meal. He'd buy and eat a whole bowl of berries and never share. Nice bread had to be as intoxicating as molasses-distilled home brew. If Cynthy had a big pot of greens with salt pork on the boil, if the hog to be eaten had a nice juicy case of fat, if sweet potatoes could be roasted in ashes, if Sunday brought biscuits with molasses and fried chicken, if someone got a mess of smelts or eels and fried em good, this was pure pleasure. He even liked a porcelain cup full of oatmeal-coloured bacon fat and fried beans drippings, not to mention oatmeal with lumps as big as eggs. George could dine on dandelion roots: they were tasty and they tasted even tastier because they were free. He chewed chocolates like pieces of steak. Once he found a sack of sugar and just ate it and ate it for days on end, secretly. Just scooped up big white handfuls and sat down in back of a shed and ate it and ate.

At fourteen, Rue convinced George to sortie with him to Halifax. They hopped the train, then trolleyed to Barrington Street, site of the swanky shops. Dressed cleanly enough so as to postpone or stymie suspicion, they entered the Homer Jewellery Store. Rue asked the owner, Mr. Homer, to show him scintillating rings so he could choose one for his gal. Smiling, grey, affable, and spectacled, Homer set the dazzling rings on the counter, while George looked nervously at Rufus. Rue eyed the display rings intently, hemming and hawing as if seriously purchasing. Then, Rue asked Mr. Homer if he could use his phone to call his bank to check on his balance. Accommodating this request, Homer ushered Rue into his back office and to his phone, then returned to the front to watch the rings and the steadily humming George. Homer and George hear Rue's loud thank-yous to his bank, and then he returns. Rufus tells Mr. Homer he will buy two rings, but not until tomorrow, once he collects his funds. Homer promises to hold the rings, and Rue and Georgie exit.

Once they are outside the shop, George says, "Rudy, ya ain't got no money for one ring, let alone two. Ya don't even got a bank account." Rue just smiles, fishes a wad of bills out of his jacket pocket.

"While that patsy was watchin ya, Joygee, I went through his safe, which was open so he could make change easily. While he thought I was brayin on the phone, I took about two hundred dollars."

George whistled, but said, "We could get jail!"

Rue peeled a twenty from his stash and handed it over. "Keep yer liver lips shut."

Rue's precocious finesse at blatant theft—bold-face and *blackface*—did not imp George to similar exploits. He felt prosperous enough, rambling amid blackberries or herding hogs. Rural life was wholesome, even if it was not, biblically speaking, holy.

George's farm work made him many things—a carpenter, a mechanic, and a gardener. But it did not make him wise or honest. He was still an amateur bootlegger, though less an expert thief. Once, though, he killed a baby bear, skinned it, and passed off the hide lucratively as fox fur.

By the time Rue was spurtin fifteen, Asa was makin his eyes very sick. When the thug lunged at Cynthy at Christmas 1941, Rufus hefted a two-by-four by the stove and whacked the sucker. Rue swung that wood till it was ruddy. Asa lunged to grab at it, but it boomeranged and smashed his nose. That hurt; then it was hard to breathe.

Cynthy screamed, "Kill him! Kill him, boy! Oh no! Don't kill him! Oh God, don't kill him, Rufus!" But Asa still stumbled bumblingly as his face collided with a hammer of wood. Asa dropped crooked, dumb—as if to apologize to that wood. Asa fell before his son's shod feet. And Rue kicked and kicked at his pops, kicked at his face. Blood come shitting out. Rue felt instantly tired. He'd hit Asa—blip!—upside the head; blood had shat out. Rue'd nearly busted his right hand on his father's steel-like head. The worse he pounded Asa, the worser his own heart pounded in return.

Asa coughed and spat, "You want to piss in my face? At it?" He'd fallen akimbo, like a sick bug. Marred and shaky, he bled onto the floor, then rose onto his haunches, and mumbled how he'd sic the cops on Rue.

Well, Rue slapped Asa's bloody face. "I'm a-gonna break ya, nigger. Ya'll wish to God ya ain't born."

Asa start to stand, spitting, "You'll not talk back. I got ya out that bitch." Asa glared at Cynthy.

But Rue roared, "Stay down there like the dog you are." He swayed like a gladiator over his hammered-down father. He just laugh, but it was a laugh that come from a gutter.

VII

N OT LONG after this thrashing, Asa disappeared into dark water—the petrol-slicked, nighttime, molasses-ebony of Halifax Harbour. It were wartime; the city housed plagues of sailors in March 1942.

Asa'd tottered from the butchery, in a patina of blood and a haze of whisky, carrying fat and spare bits of meat in a newspaper whose headlines waxed large about Stalin, Churchill, Mackenzie King, other grandiose, corpulent men. He bought a tin can of rum from a bootlegger, because he was now a drinker who ignored his alcoholism: he was always bumbling to Gabby's bar-bordello to take a taste. Asa continued lurching, shambling, homeward, a heavy-set being crunching crocus underfoot. Before he got there, he saw Reverend Dixon in his cream car, and he flagged him down; he wanted to talk to him about Cynthy and Rue and God. Dixon let the drunk man into his car, eagerly, and told him he was going to Halifax. Asa said, slurringly, "We'll have a man-to-man chat, Reverend." He fell drunkenly asleep. Dixon glanced at the snoring, slumped-down man, and said, "Cross-examine thyself." The sun criss-crossed the double-crossing road. A summery eve.

It was night when Asa awoke to find himself lying, shivering, on a wharf in downtown Halifax. He didn't much fancy the harbour—whose smell he knew instantly—because it ran with unadulterated shit, straight on into the Atlantic. Indeed, the raw sewage pipe into the harbour was Halifax's concrete answer to the Statue of Liberty, the Eiffel Tower, Big Ben, the Great Wall of China, and the Leaning Tower of Pisa. He turned his aching head and spied ruined light amid the city's ruinous streets. Whenever he'd ride the bus or train to Halifax and glimpse its entrée to the Atlantic—all that murderous water whelming, foaming, foaming, whelming—Asa would ponder his own dying, wonder how it'd go.

Dizzy and addled, Asa felt the wind tasting like rum-nectar in his paper-dry throat. A car engine wheezed and cussed nearby. Gulls wafted and squawked. He heard impetuous water glug-glugging among the wharf posts and the rock-tumbly shore. No doubt, black water was brushing boulders till they bristled black. Now and again a heavy wave'd break and snap and howl against the rocks like a whip smashing against skin. Lying by that water was the same as being rained on. Now he realized he couldn't move his arms or feet. He lifted his head and saw his limbs had been roped with chain and an ungainly bumperjack was dangling, chained to his ankles. His head was throbbing as if it had been hit with an axe, but he was conscious enough to recognize Reverend Dixon, now looming over him.

He giggled, only a little nervous, sure there was an explanation, and said, "Reverend Dixon, ain't no need to shackle me up just to get me baptized! I always been fixin on bein saved."

Dixon laughed, but muffled it with his own hand: "I'm god-damned sure you's baptized now, Asa." And then, with his feet, he nudged the prone, wriggling, now frightened man off the wharf.

Asa yelled, "Nooooo!" But he was already sinking into the water's verge, with only a soft splash. No gulls disturbed by his descent.

That night spawned a turmoil of stars. Asa was thirsty, thirsty, thirsty, then drunk, then drowning.

He died thinking, "Who's pissin in my face?" He left behind his good brown leather shoes on the wharf. His shadow had fell upon the water like an oil slick. His eyes weeping down his cheeks, his head brimming with rum, his body never found. An apparent *sans souci* suicide. He be now only a pair of brown patent leather shoes abandoned by two brown feet. So Asa sunk down, enthralled, into the cold, sloppy water. In a roomful of fish, he floated, weighted down by chains and a bumperjack. Dixon, satisfied, threw the opened newspaper package of carcass meat into the water, to deliver entertainment to the gulls—and ironic flowers to Asa. Right after Dixon drove off, a hobo named Godasse—or "dirty shoes"—swiped Asa's patent leathers.

Cynthy was comforted by Dixon. There was gossip about how Asa may have run off after Dixon had left him, kindly, in Halifax, but then Reverend Lucas of the Halifax church claimed to have seen a suicide note that had since been lost. The Mounties made inquiries, but nobody mourned Asa's absence, and so the investigation became a series of shrugs. Besides, it was wartime, and plenty of official, organized massacres was underway worldwide; a puny local death didn't interest anyone.

Assuredly, Asa's funeral was perfunctory—as were his mourners' tears. The ostensible suicide's corpse was missing, but he was far from being missed. Few felt moved to fake any sorrow on Asa's behalf, although the transports of grief staged by the presumed dead man's siblings were fearsome to behold. Thus, George and Rue experienced memorable extensions of mercy, prayer, and sympathy, along with compromisingly fond gestures, kisses, and hugs—the grace notes of gentility—from relatives. These emotive treasures befell them just because their vile papa had taken truly too much to drink, swilling saline solution in his lungs instead of alcohol in his blood. Neither brother regretted this result: for some days, they were treated like two young men with hearts and not two brutes lacking them.

Even Cynthy's tears were authentically salty, though prompted more by her tear ducts than by her heart. She accepted the fair fortune of Asa's vanishing, his deathly disappearance, with the aplomb of a cultured killer, and resolved to be a better mother since she could not be a good one. With Dixon's transportation aid, she rode triumphantly into Windsor and bought herself a red dress for revival after buying a black one for modelling grief. She suppressed any doubts about Asa's suicide, though the thought nagged her that a man so mean-spirited would wreck the world before he'd ever harm himself. But Asa was, despite all his filth, somehow cleanly gone—as if his life had been a fleck of grime that an efficient charlady had eliminated with single swish of her sopping mop. After all the grimaces, frowns, and Gothic gargoyle masks of the mourners at Asa's funeral *in absentia* (a kind of mock trial), plus her tried-and-true trysts with Dixon, Cynthy knew that, to keep her household together, she would have to kneel and go into Windsor to work "in service," as a maid, a cook, a cleaner. But this labour promised the earning of new dresses, new tickets.

George and Rue were also emancipated by Asa's finish. His absence—as good as death—left them both feeling boyish exuberance and manly possibility at once. Now they could stay up all night studying hoards of comic books; they could casually eat up what should have been Asa's share of their meals; they could sip and gulp what remained of Asa's liquor; they could breathe more easily and entertain a horizon of Aprils—thaws, buds, blooms, refreshing wind, cleansing rain…. Their muscles seemed charged with the electricity of their liberty. Their mother could upbraid their domestic laziness with glares and commands to make toil and industry their gods. They simply ignored her, pretending to honour her halo of bereavement.

Perhaps the best result of Asa's demise was that, for the first month afterwards, the slaughterhouse sent sympathy cuts of beef, pork, and lamb. For a month, the boys ate a mess of meats—chops, ham hocks, gizzards—and dreamt new plans.

Cynthy didn't long survive her husband. A stroke seized up half her once-pretty looks, gouging a half-smile into a smirk, leaving her face lopsided. Then, having taken a job in Windsor, she drooped herself over Gabby Robie's shit-blackened indoor toilet and was scrubbing and scrubbing and scrubbing away at the recalcitrant filth left by that high-class pimp's ass. She eyed a few of Robie's girls, en route to and from the marbled bathroom, but ignored Purity, who only glanced at Cynthy in passing, wondering who this twisted-up-faced Negro woman could be. It was while scouring Gabby's toilet, making it pristine, that the heart attack hit. Cynthy's fantasies of a caviar-and-truffles epoch in Montreal foundered on the reality of her gorgeous tan hands scouring a white porcelain toilet to a champagne gleam. She died dreaming of a dazzling red silk dress. She died with her eyes open. She died on her knees.

Rue and George trembled in the back room of the shack when they heard the awful voices in the kitchen, ranged around the dressed-up corpse of their mother. A dozen mourners were singing lustily after eating up a storm. Folks was cryin. Still, they had to have a drink or two. Big purple velvet drapes lay on the casket; food and flowers about. Tossed roses lay on the hard, reflecting pool of the casket. A lock of Cynthy's hair had been put in a glassed-in frame.

Alisha—imponderably old, uncowed by birth, unshaken by death—didn't give the boys more than two shakes of her head, to say "Sorry" and "Uh-huh." Reverend Dixon made promises to show up, and did so late, then made excuses to leave early.

Twelve Three Mile Plains folks was there, cryin, sniffin, singin, drinkin, eatin. They were grumpy, exotic-looking

Negro Gypsies. They were XXX Xns. But at least they cared enough for Cynthy and her bootleggin, lollygaggin, thievin survivors to show up. Not one of the dead woman's bed-friends (save Dixon) came to see her bedded down in her chaste, violet funeral gown. Her mourners and pallbearers went to her graveside strictly out of Christian charity and genealogical nostalgia. As the shabby funeral party trundled the gleaming coffin on an ox-cart to the burial ground, they passed a billboard featuring a photograph of blue-black Archie Croxen eating a red, gushing watermelon wedge and, ballooned above his head, the scarlet slogan "Windsor, N.S.: Home of Sho' Good Eatin'!"

With their whole family now a cemetery, Rue and George began to study how to live better. They'd think on it in the morning, ponder it in the evening. They could look at each other and at Three Mile Plains and see only more struggle, more suffering, more sickness. But the Not-Again World War was on, opening up jobs everywhere; the war seeded warehouses of ready caskets and treasure chests. Them days demanded the arithmetic of bullets, the mathematics of gold, the economics of theft, the accounting of farms, the finances of hunger, the statistics of labour, and the actuarial tables of killing.

To find their destinies, the stunted-hearted brothers would have to abandon the smelt snow of late April 1942. That light snow that glistened like gems. But life has no mercy for the living and no pity for the dead.

VIII

THE MA-AND-PA shack was now theirs. George assumed the coital bed, while Rue occupied solo the boyhood bed he'd shared with his brother, when they'd slept with each other's feet at the other one's head, like the inverted figures on playing cards. They kept in lots of home brew, now, distilled from hops and raisins. They kept a full keg, with a spigot on the side, sittin by the stove. Cynthy's photograph smiled lonesome and winsome down at them from the back-room wall, but Asa's pictures had long since been torn up and burnt.

That spring and summer after Cynthy's death, when they needed coin for more than just cigarettes, they'd stroll at dawn down to Newport Station and hitch the train into Windsor, hire out to haul garbage, pound nails, anything at all (but not the gypsum mine, not the knackery), then get the train back to Three Mile Plains at night, stop at Pemberton's store for groceries: chocolate bars, bubblegum, salami, cream soda, ginger ale. They'd pore over comic books too, not the newspaper. Radio blaring a crime show, crackling as if afire, they'd sit up nights, not doing much but singing, or playing harmonica, or shamefully, shamelessly sobbing, over a bootleg bottle, about being hard-done-by orphans. They hugged, sometimes, but the pain inside them tore them away from each other too.

Feeling nasty, they geared for fights always. Without explaining it to each other, and without knowing why, they'd go into

Windsor, or they'd go to Wolfville or Kentville, those cigarette or liquor towns, shuttling between Three Mile Plains and Kentville, either hitchhiking or going by train, but set to fight: white boys, mixed-up boys, black boys. Didn't matter. They wanted to incubate *Fear* for miles around. They wanted to be hulking hundred-plus-pound holy horrors. They wished to be so sharp-eyed, so quick in hand they could dice air with a razor, cleave the wings off a fly in mid-flight. They'd pick a town, go and get uncomfortably drunk, then comfortably snooze in an apple orchard, then walk back to town for more rum. They'd drink away whole weekends in the Annapolis Valley, keel over, then get up, set to tussle.

One July, Saturday night, the guys was staggerin back across a railroad bridge from Kentville when three chalk-faced toughs blocked their passage on that narrow bridge.

The palefaces laughed, "Let's crunch these nigguhs up." Rue already had em measured.

George told em boys, "I been drinkin and am feelin kinda tired. So I'm gonna let my brother handle yas, while I sit down and rest." Woozily, George sat down beside the tracks, while Rue made three guys feel sorry for themselves. One by one, he ground each of those white boys—well-done, medium, and rare.

Then George, sobered now, got up, said, "My turn!"

He smacked the trio silly while the sweaty, panting Rue shouted, "Run em down, knock em down, and kick em. Hard! Pound piss out of em! Break their spirits!"

IX

THE APRIL after Cynthy was buried, sixteen-year-old Rufus, returning from another Valley dust-up, plus happy helpings of rum, passed a wooden, red-tint, square house anchoring Panuke Road. A girl-woman stuck her head out a window, purely coincidentally, and he just up and kissed her—in dawn-crisp air, flourishing light. That gal's face was like a bouquet, so cinnamon-and-pepper beautiful. She tried to slap Rue, but he ducked, laughed.

Said, "Ya look just too pretty. Is I too bold?"

Easter Jarvis said, "Sorry bout yer Mama, but ya shouldn't be kissin on a gal who don't know ya."

Rue said, "Lemme know you then." He was hungry to be the first and last man to feel Easter.

Easter was a plum good gal, plump and sweet, her glistening, chestnut-coloured hair framing caramel looks: pacific skin riding coral that was bones. Her waist be so small, Rue could scope one hand around that sweetness, feel her hair strokin down like black vines. He was starving for fruitful trees alive with blossoms.

Easter and Rue stuck together instantly. Rue planned to quit scrappin, toing-and-froing anywhere, drinkin. He had to get out into the world, away from Three Mile Plains, with a gal he could trust. Easter's daddy was a railway porter who'd lavished cash on her and her mom. She wanted to become a nurse—when Coloured girls could. She wished to move to Halifax, work hard, buy a comfy house, have oodles of kids. Rufus thought he might become a pianist-porter—or porter-pianist. He loved the luxury of that dream as much as he loved Easter. He'd become a sleeping-car porter for the Canadian National Railway. (Coloureds called it the Canadian Negro Railway because it employed Canadian Negroes as porters. The Canadian Pacific Railway was called the Coloured Peoples Railway because it hired West Indians, Negro Americans, and "real" Indians.) They knew the facts: men had to porter, women launder. Men would go away all week on long runs to Montreal; women'd take in soiled clothes one day, return them all washed and ironed the next.

That society, organized to drive coal-coloured men into laborious destitution, was a gigantic and depressing frustration for Rue. He was not one to embrace hard luck with a happy-go-lucky smile. But Easter's optimism, her graces of cradling kisses, her family's plucky stick-to-itiveness, helped steel Rue's belief he could prosper as a musician, train man, husband, father, *provider*; that he could be an artist, not just artful.

Ah, Easter be easy to love. And look at the season! The spring brandishing blossoms; the sun-singed snow retreating. Rue craved to draw Easter into hyacinths, with the moon gone vermilion some misty summer night.

Easter was the antidote to cold soup.

Rue jest with her: "It's chocolate that makes Easter Easter—the chocolate hens, bunnies, and eggs, *not* the sermons." Easter'd hit im with her handbag to strike down irreligion. They'd tussle, cuddle, kiss. But all weren't ideal. When they took in a movie, Easter had to take out her cash. If Rue wanted a tub of ice cream, he had to let Easter pay.

Rue fell into a fight right on Main Street in Windsor, and it was over Easter. He caught that whoremaster, Gabby Robie, actin fresh with her. Well, in the sunlit street, Rue plastered Gabby flat on his nose; the blood just flew. The wrinkled-up old hunchback bitched, but Rue kept circlin and boxin his head. Gabby wobbled, backed off.

A witness yelled, "I got in the barber chair when you fellas started fightin and my hair was all cut when ya stopped." Easter gratefully kissed Rue long and hard.

Still, Easter was one of the "400s"—one of those better-off Negroes who had houses, new clothes, flash, big words, cars (or horses), quiet gumption, RESPECT, gardens, white friends, and style, but who kept their furniture covered up in sheets to preserve the newness. Easter was meant to marry within her set. But Rue's kiss put him in sole contention for her honours—and her savings, though her pa, Loquinn, cringed at the very name of this ragamuffin. Loquinn was stocky, light-complected, and bulldog-mean, but a tony railway porter; Easter was headstrong, and his only child. Loquinn hated Rue as if he had always known him.

Easter had a piano in her parlour. When her folks'd go out, she let Rue play that half a keyboard he knew, then she'd serve him her good food: cabbage, turnip, carrot, squash, and eels too. Rue loved buttermilk and fried eels. He watched those darned things flapping around in Easter's frying pan after being prepared and floured. Then he and Easter shared red wine and kisses. She served Rue easy turtle cookies and Halifax rice pudding. She'd hoist white stockings on her honey legs— just for him. They dreamt of a Christmas of cheese, champagne, and chocolates, not to mention an adulthood of babies, blues piano, and brandy. With Easter, Rue felt he could play an apple-pie hero with bread-and-butter proverbs.

He mused, "One day, I'll sleep side her every night."

Rue said to Easter in December, "We need a driving horse. Can't always walk or cab. With a horse, you can ride out, see me up home." Easter's doting pa purchased a black filly, Andover, as a Christmas gift. Loquinn swallowed—like bad rum—his distaste for Rue, who was, to him, one more no-good Negro who gave all the hard-working ones a bad name. But Loquinn bought the sable mare, to tether her in his barn, to tether Easter, he hoped, to his home.

That Christmas was the best Rue ever had, with Easter prancing on her horse, and him and her cavorting and not caring who knew. She gave Rufus chocolates, cheese, champagne, and a new belt with a silver buckle. He gave her kisses and promises of kisses. He played her a song using only half her piano.

The ice on the Avon River was deadly in winter, but now the new spring fields were blurry with melting April snow, and the ice had to burst open in pieces. A high spring tide made the Avon a squall of water. The Atlantic, corkscrewing into the Bay of Fundy and churning into the Minas Basin, turned the Avon into a plough of water that could tear down and smash up iron bridges in that April of 1944. One year after Rue first kissed Easter.

Easter'd arranged to meet Rue at three, atop the hill where the rich had erected mansions under Windsor elms. While awaiting her arrival from Falmouth, Rue eyed cars and horses-and-buggies passing by, in front of the Windsor Baptist Church, the granite white church that spurned the wooden African Baptist facility up home. It was an easy landmark for downtown meetings. The sky was a grey-white-black watercolour turning to oils, and the wind seemed to come from January, not April. It whipped back and forth, careening, cold, mixing flecks of snow with specks of rain. But Rue felt gleeful. He could hardly wait to clasp Easter inside his coat against him, to breathe her breath like hot chocolate and to feel her breasts pressing softly into him. They'd sip hot chocolate downtown, then ride slowly to the Plains. Then the squall blew in his face and reminded him he was poor and subject to the atmosphere's whims.

Easter was riding Andover across the spindly, rickety wooden Avon River bridge—when the river erased that bridge. Only its approaches remained, leaping expectantly toward a void. Pitched into that agitated chrome, Easter tried to keep ahold of Andover, but the horse flailed, the avalanche of ice and water burying Easter in her long black coat and apple-blossom-coloured spring dress. She almost swam, but the water was too slippery for traction and too cold to stand. It was slob water, a slushy mess of water, ice, half-frozen snow, and mud. One wild, freakish black wave had shook Easter from Andover. The next wave, quadrupling up on the first, became her assassin. It was a cyclone of water, boulders, logs, mud, and ice crashing down on anything already drowning. She somersaulted through the crushing water. Dirt and frozen water besmirched her clean, dry lungs. The sad, slow ache of disaster overtook her. She saw water turning white, as if with ice, then blackness, as she drowned, gurgling. Her eyes rimed with sand pretending to be stars. The sun rose to paleness, incandescent, as water blanketed her head and she settled, shivering, into a bed of shells and amethysts.

Rudy waited in that drenching chill and icy buffeting for an hour. Then he went to meet Easter. When he reached the Avon River, he saw the bridge drifting, tumbling, bobbing, in bits and pieces, trusses and spans, dismantled among pies and strudels of ice. Rue joined the ragtag throng gazing upon the ruins, but still felt only tiny anxiety. Surely Easter had postponed her travel, or had ridden to a safer passage, although Rue knew there was no good place to cross: the river, with all that jagged ice, was a cocktail of glittering razors. He squinted into the distance, among the empty orchards of Falmouth, looking for a brown girl on a black horse, while the ice groaned and heaved practically at his feet.

He was scanning the horizon when he heard a snake-like voice tut-tutting, "I seen the Jarvis gal go down when the bridge went out. Her and her horse." Rue twisted about sharply to face that vile voice, to smack Gabby's face.

But murmuring others grabbed, clutched, held his arms, as he heard Gabby say, with a ghost of a smile, "I seen her go in— and her horse—more than an hour ago, and that's that."

Rue sweated panic that let him slip the hands gripping him and stab-punch at the grotesque man who crowed, "If she'd worked for me, she'd still be alive." Gabby crumpled while the crowd yammered, and Rue bolted to the riverbank. Light drained from the heavens. A cold rain lashed and pummelled.

Dazed, but hoping dreadfully that Easter might yet be floating on a floe like an Eskimo heroine or, maybe, lying ashore, half-drowned, exposed to freezing cold in her sodden clothes, Rufus rushed to Easter's house to augment a search party. A crowd mobbed the kitchen. He pushed through the tumult of sobbing and serious-faced people.

Loquinn spied Rue; he picked up a butcher knife and swung, screaming, "You's to blame for this! Ya told Easter to get that horse!" Loquinn slashed at the air in front of Rue while folks in the kitchen jumped back. Rue grabbed the crying, yelling man's wrist and squeezed harshly until the knife hit the floor and Rue kicked it aside. He turned and left, and just wept and wept and wept.

Searchers dragged the Fundy water and patrolled the rain-hiked river from cliffs, seeking Easter. They sloshed around boulders of muddy, muddy ice on the riverbanks.

Later, she washed up by Evangeline Beach among seaweed-laced rocks. Her body had been dissolving in water. A lovely, delicate, easy sculpture of flesh and bone had been chafed to and fro in pulverizing, fretting tides.

Where Easter is buried, on a slope above the Minas Basin,

the sky scowls over the sea—breakers seething home. It is whitewashed, blizzarding air. A broken heavens. A snow-stung sky. Her stone is white granite confronting whiter waves.

Her mama, Delicia, said, through a waterfall of tears, "People don't know how good my daughter was. Pure her body was."

X

AFTER EASTER S DEATH, Rue could not tolerate the rose smell, the apple blossom aromas, the peach scents of Three Mile Plains.

He said, "I must start out and scythe down grass for myself."

He boarded the train to Halifax, that open sewer on the Atlantic. Its alleys unfurled a parade of puddles and garbage and feces and head-dented cats. Dogs looked half-run-over or had only three legs. Ugly gals sashayed with black-leather-skirted asses or black-silk-scarved necks. Salubrious, unchaste voices, redolent of pigeon squabble and pidgin gabble, chortled over sidewalks scrawled on by illiterate Satanists whose graffiti exclaimed, "Satin lives!" Pigeons stumbled like broken-winged rats at Haligonian feet. Always, clouds clung to the city, for it liked to have its sunlight shrouded in fog.

Was an operatic city, Halifax, with Citadel Hill splitting it between the smokestack North End and the rose-trellised South. A peninsula, its shape resembled the cranium of a *Tyrannosaurus rex*. Streets were haphazardly flung, ragged daggers, plunging downhill to the harbour or stabbing uphill, then vaulting past the domineering Citadel and the flat, adjacent Commons, to dart downhill again to the Northwest Arm or Bedford Basin. It were a San Francisco of vice with San Franciscan hills. Easy for a car to conk out when moving uphill, then roll speedily backwards, right down into the harbour. Many a horse had met its end because some gentleman's flivver had struck it as the vehicle hurtled unstoppably backwards into disaster.

Halifax was the Warden of the North, a fast, filthy city, warships bustling about the perpetually pro-war harbour, a clapboard London of booty. It had never recovered from its abandonment by the British Empire. The city imagined its obsolescent cannon and superseded forts still guarded the Arctic, thus keeping those waters technically British, despite the Yanks' ungodly firepower. Halifax was Venice without canals, Kingston with mosquitoes. It was the Sodom of the Atlantic—a gold mine of prostitution. Every day, atop the Citadel, punctiliously at noon, a single cannon blast marked the city's further passage into history. Even antichrist Hitler pipe-dreamed about commandeering an ale-profit-built South End château for himself.

Here the war was going kapow, kapow, kaboom, kapow, whammy, every day in the Loyal press, and markets were crowded with khaki'd soldiers and white-uniformed sailors desperate for swell satisfactions before sailing to battles in Europe—and also the Battle of the Atlantic, just to get to the main war. In Hell-of-a-Fuck, they saw that even chubby gals had pretty legs. They wanted to live a little before, unluckily, dying, for the Atlantic bristled with U-boats deep-sixing Allies and millions of tonnes of shippage. Under such conditions, religion was ridiculous. The true holy sites were the bars, the brothels, the taverns. Vice meant steady work. Houses were quickly organized—cop-okayed—on Brunswick, Agricola, and Gottingen, near the naval base of Stadacona, all working-class, mapled, and trolleyed streets, sliding into, or rising slowly from, the never-freezing, a-hundred-ships-at-a-time whoring harbour.

The good news about all that huffing-and-puffing Haligonian prostitution was that the instant, upward spike in v.d. infections prompted public health officials to organize sex hygiene classes and adult learning campaigns. War plus lechery equalled improved literacy, but unimproved minds.

The city's Negro district, Africville, occupied the south side of Bedford Basin, on the peninsula's North End tip. Though its denizens had land titles granted by Victoria herself, the city council considered the seaside village a shantytown fit only for a slaughterhouse, railway tracks, a tuberculosis and polio hospital, and the city jail. The Coloureds in Africville wouldn't let in shifty interlopers who might give its citizens black eyes and bad names. Rue was welcome to play cards and buy bootleg, but he weren't welcome to stay.

Rue tried the railways, but couldn't get on with either company: the waiting list for portering was eight-hundred Coloured guys long. He could go to war—that is, he could go peeling potatoes in the Royal Canadian Navy, serving *dummkopfs* who'd call him nigger while gobbling his hash browns and sausages. There'd be fights; he'd be brigged and discharged, if he weren't shot. Not for him.

Having gone from Three Mile Plains to drunkenness, and from there to Halifax, Rue, now a beanpole seventeen-year-old, wandered the codfish-perfumed and Moir's-chocolate-factory-scented downtown streets. Soon, he landed a piano gig in a Brunswick Street bordello run by a "malloto" guy with tabby-cat skin and a face like malt, name of Googie Johnson, right from Africville. Googie was hefty, diamonded, silk-suited, coiffed, with a scar all the way round one eye and down one cheek. That warned that anyone who jousted with him could get his testicles ripped off. He'd broken both his hands—twice—tussling with fools and smashing down doors. But he was still pretty. When he wanted another man's woman, he'd just look at her and she'd come right over: better that than see her man sliced up like a filet. His English was just spat-out tobacco juice. Few fathomed it, which was the point. It was always evening in his establishment's plush innards—to help soldiers, sailors, as well as South End business types forget their mortality and marriages. Its slick—or plump—girls were refugees from fatal mills or repulsive fathers or hellfire faiths. They were tawny and leonine and maple and mahogany and ebony and ivory and pine and mauve like dusk and peach-cream and teak and coconut and rosy and brass and bronze and cream. They were Ethiopian or Asiatic lovelies with Abyssinian or Arabian accents. To Googie, women, black or white, were like clouds, soft outside but full of turmoil inside. Blues be in them just like blues—saturating, marinating, tissues and organs, everything, in a brine of tears, vodka, and vinegar, resulting in piquant sex and gourmet music. Googie had few cop hassles: the wages of vice is profit.

Rue got outfitted for his new *rôle*: a black suit ($20), a black overcoat ($15), and a pair of black dress shoes ($10). He had to jettison the look and smell of the hayfields. It was a way to forget Easter, to forget Three Mile Plains. Rue ached to be spiffy, a nappy Napoleon, with maybe a flower in one lapel. He'd become an expert in the way to wear a tie that's shiny, the way to make sure the suit drops right, just right, around the frame, the way to wear shoes that are natty, snazzy, and jet-spanking black. He knew now how to hold a cigarette, how to wear a hat—with gangster poise. Still, Rue had a handicap: he knew how only half the piano sounded. The first half of the keyboard was constantly fooling and shocking him with its heavy, sable, deep bass notes, too resonant, and so he nixed all requests. All his pieces were originals: he had no repertoire. His blues was, thus, immaculately pure jazz, improv, boogie freestyle. Who could dance to it? All Rufus could produce was "Amazing"-ly broken "Grace," or a series of sliding and bucking notes that harmonized like jagged carpentry. His funeral songs sounded like up-tempo ragtime. Rue put on disconcerting concerts. His style was not unpleasant, but also not pleasing. His notes were real notes—you could feel em indigoing air. Pasty Dalhousie frat boys cottoned on to Rue's style. It were "nifty" how he squeezed so much enriched pain into the sarcophagus of a piano. Fans could sniff the phosphorous glint of jazz in the dark, opaque notes. But they could not spend much money. So this praise of Rue was, to Googie, spittle. His eyes squished into a squint. To Googie, Rue beat the keyboard like he was knockin out a motherfucker's brains. Most pianists felt a tune; Rue hammered em out.

Rue's gig paid off princely—ten bucks a week plus drinks. But his playing didn't inspire dancing, drinking, coupling, tippling, or any of the merrymaking that should accompany money-making. Rather, Rufus's pianist style forced everyone to just stand around sipping, pondering, as if attending a recital instead of revelling in a blind pig and cathouse. The piano was spooky; its music haunted every room in the house, messin up lovers' rhythms.

To step outside this night-owl hangout was to step into a nightmare: a tableau of drunks pissing against walls; smoky, poxy apocalyptic gals; a couple screwing in a dark doorway. Worse, at times it was Rue himself taking advantage of poor woodsmoke-scented, stove-oil-perfumed quim, some thin-titted slut, a long plaid shirt and a tartan skirt camouflaging the conjunction. A favour for a fiver.

Then, at Googie's, Rue met Purity Mercier, down from Windsor to slip the Mounties. He didn't want her: his heart was still mash. The coupling was chancy. Rue'd stood up, turned from the piano, not noticing Purity, but holding a cup of coffee. As he turned, he spilled into her; the coffee trembled, leapt in the cup, splashed out urgently—but not scaldingly—upon her bare white arm. She laughed; her hands lolled over her now sheerly visible breasts. Wasn't Rue like a Coloured man she'd funned with up in Windsor? Her nervous, brittle laughter revealed little pleasant incisors as biting as her looks. Her feverish mouth, snatching. She thought Rue swarthy and, therefore, randy. His eyes murderously brilliant, volcanic. There was no membrane of glass dividing them, only stained-glass lust inside Rufus. She seemed cutely ratty, acutely dirty. The colour and taste of vodka and milk. Dark-haired Purity'd fit his narrow bed.

She say, "I come from two lines of whores, and I'm a whore myself." Rue was the bull to trample in her garden, kick in her stall, chew on her roses. Fine, fine.

Their affair had *lust* in it—the remains of *lustre*. Her fingers diddling along his spine reminded Rue of a roach's legs paddling furiously in Googie's sink. When they turned up the lamp, yellow light, half-religious, half-sinful, all shames assumed a Renaissance glow—beige, peaceful. The bed cracked and jiggled as they cranked and joggled. Her sluice suckled him.

"Oh—what—ah." Fire sat within Purity, burning, burning, in her succinct precincts. Either like a preacher's abandoned sermon, her skirts' undone, or like a bad nun's, with unchaste heart and unbound hair.

Purity was Rue's lover under tall pines in Point Pleasant Park, down by the waterfront, in late June, after the shower, pouring rain down her trembling self and gyrating amid the mud and pine needles. Tangy skin, vinegary kisses, sour wet clothes peeled off in all that rain and mud. They'd done it standing in the doorless changing room while slummy water gummed up the dry sand by the black harbour, with cold strawberries and stars and rain-sodden, wind-slurred grass in the nearby hills. The Sunday chill thrilled through June leaves. Rum hammering in Rue's head hammered him to Purity's thighs. Then, wet, panting, the lovers sheltered in one of the mouldered caverns of one of the ancient imperial forts. They dressed; Rue hummed. He desired the hectic Atlantic spray on their faces. Purity smiled. Rue remembered Easter and brushed away a threatening tear.

The intimates—inmates of intimacy—rested until an orange moon yellowed toward white; then, they left. Purity's almost blissful perfume mingled with the salt-and-grease smell of fish 'n' chips up by the Commons. Drunks lounged and slept on the grass as if it were a divan. The night was sable indigo; their shadows moved black under streetlamps bent over them like sodomite monks.

Rue dreamt of how nice it'd be to smash flies' soft bodies against Purity's hard, sober whiteness, to make it darker, softer. He wondered if Purity, plastered with hundreds of corpses of smeared flies, might seem delectably darker. He dreamt of the little ivory tub she liked to wash her little ivory sex in, while sitting in the lascivious posture of a cedilla. Silk rippling black down white legs.

In Purity's eyes, Rue's a kind of crow, raven, vulture, vampire, as black as rat's fur. He could half play the piano and pretend to play the rest. When he was in her, in her bed, the air they breathed was like sticky slime.

They were lying in bed, joined at their hips, on the always-seditious Dominion Day night, with fireworks fluting and bursting seditiously over the usually blacked-out wartime city, when Purity joked about a comical fella who'd tried to get her to carry his child. "His name was Asa. He look like you."

With dreadful ice in his heart, Rue knew he was embedded in Asa's whore. He drilled deeper, harder. Having her was like having revenge, and having it blisteringly cold. He heard Asa giggling in the shadows. He pulled out of Purity's lap, then hit her. Once, twice, thrice.

Three slaps to get blood oozing from her lips, and she was yelling, "Blackbastardfuckinblackbastard." Rue swore he'd bash Purity until she was his colour. He grabbed his belt out his pants. He was gonna whip impure Purity with the silver buckle Easter'd given him. Purity hollered, and Googie burst in: the glass of the door broke in a star-shape. He slugged hard; his fists struck oil with each connection; Rue folded onto the Turkish carpet.

Googie loathed commotion and upset—and he hated Rue's unfunky jazz: music should doctor, not need one. Haps Rue forgot he was only a half-ass hayseed, only half a pianist, and a dime-a-dozen. Ergo, the sucker'd have to square up, clear out, pronto. Rue'd get a few bucks, and then the door. Googie couldn't abide no nigger ignoramus!

XI

AFTER Easter'd drowned, Rufus was impossible to endure. To George, it seemed his family was just mortally bad news. To stick with Rue could mean, then, his own doom. It was time to escape. Georgie knew there was about a hundred dollars of insurance money in the shack; he'd torch the shack, collect the moolah, split it, bill for bill, with Rue, and they'd skedaddle different routes. He set the fire, saw Cynthy's photo blaze, got the cash, gave Rue almost half.

Georgie left Three Mile Plains but chose to stay in Windsor because he liked country life. He did odd jobs for Pius Bezanson, a farmer, for ten bucks a month. Not sour pay, compared with bitter poverty. Bezanson's belief was, "Let every man turn *pain* into bread." Bezanson let George bunk in the barn, where he managed to snore despite stench and noisy, beastly copulations of animals. Mosquitoes were also wicked, stabbin George relentlessly. Even so, Georgie felt he'd do better, by and by. Hope was as striking as lightning, as deep as water, water, water, and as dream-productive as rum.

Farmin was natural for Georgie, and Bezanson let him eat and eat. Once, the farmer paid Georgie with a seven-pound tin of blueberry jam, seven loaves of bread, and seven quarts of rum. Georgie made rum and jam sandwiches. Some good under crow-fractured, dark-blue Heaven. He had to wade through bushes, spend days cutting poplar trees and maples and spruce and pine. He could milk cows, churn cream, set out eggs delicate, delicate. He'd lead oxen—and, times, get bogged down in mud. He could tiptoe through the marsh bushes, the thinner woods near the Avon River, tumble into orange-red mud and climb out, or quickly skinny-dip in the river. He'd wander, separate, alone, among lichened rocks, let salt spray off the Fundy splash his Coloured Nova Scotian face. He'd take barrels and haul apples out the trees. He could drink fresh water by scooping up rain. A downy rain could make even October taste as fresh as April. After trainloads of apples, after muddy roads.

He'd found Paradise. Now he needed a woman.

From this farm at Windsor's edge, George eyed, daily, passing, dairy girls, lasses only thirteen or twelve, perched upright, like postage stamp queens, atop small, slow Percherons. The girls'd titter, chatter, sing. Jostling, their dairy pails pinged, as jittery as kindling breaking into flame. The dames gleamed unusually beautiful; their Madonna-like smiles as gay as fresh milk. George watched em giggle, shout, sing, as they'd pass by him on the Orotava Road. He juggled blue plums to entice their eyes. They'd look back, teehee, and he felt gratified. He noticed Blondola—one of the solar-eclipsing Plains belles (from Englishman River Falls)—noticing him. Georgie chase her small horse and hand her a blue plum. Blondola smiled, and he felt melted. She was like a fat, plush mare. The pretty women'd rub berry juice on their lips. Blondola too. The blacker the berry, the sweeter the juice. Blondola was thirteen, but plump, bodacious. A lively-lookin, dark-skinned black girl in black. Her face was chocolate smooth, with supremely plush, violet lips. Her coal-coloured eyes were lit up as if by an internal night of stars. Just her "Hi," the way she'd say it, 'd jolt Georgie's heart. Maybe they'd be so much in love that, making love, they'd feel like they were equally his and hers, that one set of hands was as dependable as the other. Ah, that chocolate-dark, chocolate-sweet woman, her plum-tint eyes!

> *The road is all dirt—dirty,*
> *My gal is all pert—pretty.*

Blondola was authoritatively everything Georgie wanted: her deep laughter reminded him of the scary gaiety of Cynthy's laughter when she was sweaty-happy with Asa.

Georgie study Blondola close.

He ask, "How ya get that name, Blondola? Ya a secret movie star?"

She be bashful: "Nah, Ma's name be Cassie and ma aunt's Ann, so my middle name's Cassandra."

Georgie get avid: "And Blondola?" Blondola just laugh and go on her way, gigglin with the other maids. They tease Georgie fierce.

One joked, "Men peacocks are more colourful than girl ones."

Blondola yelled, "If only it were like that with our men!"

Blondola looked a super good woman, with her plaid lumber-jack shirts and jackets, her stories based on recipes, her country blues radio curing tobacco. She was partial to a house with sun in the living room and smelts drying on the roof; to a dunga-reed Romeo. Like everybody in Three Mile Plains, she'd grown up with blues gossip bout lethal booze; bout buttoned-down, open-flied preachers; bout leathered-down cowboys mangled by gypsum-mine dynamite. She'd be happy to go along with a man, a man goin somewhere, somewhere far.

Courtin Blondola should've been easy for Georgie. She liked his drawl, his laugh, his fearless—and sober—hard work. But he was hindered in his interest because he had no place to bring Blondola. The big drafty, stinky barn he slept in was no site for wooin a swell young gal makin dove's eyes at him. Georgie'd've to pull down better than ten bucks a month to be an effective Casanova.

He found a dream solution. He saw a newsreel about khaki-clad Canucks crossin the Atlantic to cross swords with Hitler, boys clearly no taller, bigger, or older than him. They appeared on the movie screen, silvery and sunny, smokin on the Halifax docks, waitin to board ships, and kissin on two delicious gals each. All Georgie knew of war was what funny books showed: a lot of rat-a-tat-tat and pow and splat and whammy. But maybe he could ship overseas, kill a clutch of Krauts, bulk up into a he-man, lift gold rings off married corpses, juxx some British quim, then return, swaggering, and marry Blondola with much hoopla—with their wedding pix in the *Hants County Register*. He'd seize his future this way.

So George told Blondola he was goin to the Boches-Hun War, and he ask, "Will ya wait for me?" He'd enlist, return, keep her glad. Blondola was playful, gleeful, but found Georgie spellbindingly earnest. She nodded; they kissed.

XII

EIGHTEEN now, George didn't have to lie about his age to get into the Canadian Active Army, but still he ask a black woman—Naomi Jones, who was as blind as water—to go to the recruiters and claim to be his mother and vouch for his age. George told recruiters he was born in the United States, Massachusetts, Boston. (Because Naomi knew about Georgie's sorry childhood, she never interrupted with any truth.)

So George pressed himself on the service and—after he was stripped and checked for lice—got pressed into service at once, peelin tatoes, slingin hash, scourin honey buckets. Yessum, he then wondered if he'd die like Cynthy, scrubbing latrines. The valiant cook and heroic janitor endured the rigmarole of "bastard training" up in Sorel, P.Q. (by the Historic Murder Site of Kamouraska), where Frenchies dubbed him Joe Louie, and he'd have to cook em all hash after, like them, he'd run five miles (fully geared up), crawled through mud, hurled himself past barbed-wire barricades, and dug foxholes. But white boys got to play cards and harmonica after; the Indian and the Coloured, well, they still had to fry eggs and swab barracks. Still, though George was Grade-A Infantry meat, when all his comrades got shipped out—to slog up and through Italy and hand out maple syrup as well as copies of *Anne of Green Gables* in Italian—George's name weren't in that number. No, his weapons would be a mop, a broom, a paring knife. Georgie hated "blaytent prejadis," so he walk away from Camp No. 45, went AWOL. He still wanted, somehow, to be a notched-gun hero, not a potato peeler.

Georgie boarded a train to Montreal, Cynthy's fabled city. After ogling the glorious Sepia Showgirls (some looked hauntingly like his ma) and gobbling smoked meat on rye with a dill pickle, he bought a black-market registration card for five dollars and signed up with the Merchant Marine as Cliff Croxen.

The ship he engaged with, in August 1944, was the S.S. *Karma* owned by Newton and Tuttles out of Yorkshire, Hull, England. His job was to stoke the boilers. To shovel coal. That was all, but he was still literally going somewhere. Aboard this seemingly divinely shielded vessel, George even got to see Siberia, voyaging through the icefields thereabouts very, very slowly, while serenading his buddies on his Dante harmonica. But when he was in London, the "Ol' Country," between the ale and the strippers, he never saw sweet fuck-all. But it was good, it was jolly cheerio splendid, to inhale British exhaust and hear pub Billingsgate on the Kraut-cratered, bomb-blasted streets. Best thing was fish 'n' chips, wet, moist, tangy with salt and vinegar, with brown ale that tasted like a cross between vinegar and molasses. A scuffle in a pub got Georgie skirmishin with bobbies, and he got tossed in jail for a week. Visited by the Sally Ann, he spent his time toying with *The Scofield Reference Bible*, while dreaming of playing with a Scofield gun.

Georgie never see any direct action. Closest he got was on the high ocean, crossing water way too heavy to be sky, way too light to be land, his skin reflecting the iridescent Atlantic. The first time he crossed the North Atlantic, he saw waves ten storeys high and could hold nothing in his stomach, and it was only vomit, vomit, vomit, for three unholy days. When he got used to the thunderous heaving of the Atlantic, he viewed three scrap-metal reefs of bursting, burning ships, and blazing sailors, some of them jumping into an ocean surfaced by flames. It was horrible: the screams of the cremating; the moans of the drowning. A sinking ship was a big mass grave dug by a torpedo. After those banshee detonations, bits of jumbled crews would bob in the water: a hand, a torso, a head and part of a shoulder. Water resembled a huge mess of half-digested meals. Corpses'd litter a midnight sea. Some would float into port, all the way back to Halifax, arriving, stately, as truncated, battered logs. Dispirited, brine-sodden, skeletal.

Once, Georgie saw shrapnel hit a shipmate. The sailor's skull opened like a watermelon. His shocked eyes popped out like corks. He couldn't believe he was dead. He laughed: that's when the blood came out in a rush and he fell smack over-board. One of ten thousand heroes buried in water.

When the Europe War shut down, George exited the Merchant Marine. He was paid three hundred bucks and discharged. But as soon as he came ashore, George was arrested by military police from the no-longer-zombified Canadian Army and, treated as a deserter, was tossed in the brig. He sat there for twenty-eight days while the army evaluated his faculties and the facts. He'd been a deserter for over two hundred days. What was his fucking problem, exactly? First, he was "Colored" or "Dark" ("Complexion") with "Brown Eyes" and "Black Hair" and holding the "Trade" of "Heavy Labourer," whose official function in His Majesty's Canadian Army was only as "General Duty." He also had a "tattoo right forearm ins. G.H." that he'd picked up in London. He also claimed incredibly to have travelled to South America, North Africa, England, and Siberia, and that the S.S. *Karma*'d been bombed twice. ("No record of any such blasted incidents.")

Jaundiced, the army decided to fire a "negro" who wouldn't mop floors or crack eggs without whining. So George's conduct was summed up as "Bad," and he was discharged on a "10-29-10" (R.O. 1029 [10]), meaning he was "Unable to meet the required military physical standards" and was "Unlikely to become an efficient soldier." Medically speaking, George seemed fine. The army doc deemed him a "young negro well developed and nourished and talkative, loquacious, cheerful, and friendly," with only a few carious teeth, no scoliosis in his spine, no local tenderness or weird masses in his stomach, and no murmurs in his heart, and with symmetrical lungs, a normal pharynx and tonsils, and a regular pulse.

But the army shrink specified that George had a "Psychopathic Personality" with "a negative attitude toward the army," that he complained often of headaches, that he'd had chicken pox in childhood, and that he'd been tossed into detention for two days in Sorel, P.Q., because of robbery: "he stole money from a Cpl. Belliveau, contrary to military law." George was also of "doubtful stability," showed "undisciplined behaviour," had a record of "tremendous job shifting, doing odd jobs everywhere on farm and in the bush," expressed "a lack of grit-guts," swore to "some trouble with army policy for little trouble," and, lying, said, "I never drink. Never smoke." In total, G.H. was a "childish negro, an unhappy man who cannot get along with other people." True: he was an "inadequate liar" whose "affirmations often appear unbelievable." Asked if he had any complaint about his medical dossier, George wrote, "Nothing." Georgie signed off on his receipt of "all my Pay, Allowances, and Clothing," and then Private G. A. Hamilton, once of the No. 6 District Depot, either in Halifax, N.S., or in the Cape Breton Highlander Reserve, was dismissed. *At-ten-shun!*

XIII

T HE ARMY head shrink had recommended Hamilton
return to the Merchant Marine because that would
"satisfy your impulsive adventuresome temperament"
or, if not that, do "heavy outdoor labour under supervision."
But Georgie recollected Montreal as the last place he'd been
borderline happy before joining the Murder Marine. He also
wanted, desperately, to collect some collateral before wooing
Blondola again and wedding her now.

So Georgie boarded the *Ocean Limited* and clickety-clacked
northwest to that Paris of the Saint Lawrence: Montreal. That ex-
fur-trade, beaver-pelt metropolis boasted Coloured bars,
Coloured dancers, brown-sugar beauties, and brown-sugar
dandies. Strolling Sainte-Catherine Street at night was like prom-
enading an avenue of tinfoil and diamonds. Georgie enjoyed
peeking inside theatrical clubs that were hot-pink and basic-black
boxes, featuring "exotic" lovelies—spun-candy fancies—from
the Quebec heartland who hoped to be discovered and delivered
to sophisticated, vulgar Hollywood but who usually got discovered in someone's husband's arms and then delivered to a hospital on a stretcher. Georgie figured his army service, though spent
in the brig, could gain him a bouncer post, even if he was more
suited for pitching hay than he was for pitching drunkards.

After a week of ambling Montreal's steep streets, eating the
usual smoked meat sandwiches with garnishes of dill pickle,

with nightly adventures among the willing dancers, George got himself a nightclub job, Rue-like, at Le Sphinx. His position was not front-line, however. The white male clientele would not tolerate a Coloured bouncer but could not object to a Coloured dishwasher. Here George's army service helped him spectacularly: he had rare experience in washing dishes, glasses, cutlery, and so he reddened his tan hands in scalding, foaming water while scouring beer, wine, and martini glasses mainly. (Almost nobody ate anything on the night shifts.) One fringe pleasure for Georgie was getting to hear musicians playing their striptease music and getting to hear raucous men's dirty encouragements, voiced in French and English, to their entertainers to parade extra-extravagantly across the dingy stage.

Just like in the army, George could provide invisible benefits to others, but could not extract any for himself, beyond the meagre pay the nightclub owners flipped his way in the form of grimy coins. It was hardly serious money, and so, just as he used to pilfer from his army buddies at basic training in Sorel, so now he took to wandering the deserted 2 a.m. streets of the metropolis with a jeweller's hammer, screwdriver, and flashlight. He could tap a window just enough to shatter it, plunder cigarettes, chocolate bars, and other goods quick and easy to sell, or even jimmy a back door to a business to snatch up anything he could, hoping against hope against the possibility of guard dogs or burglar alarms or aroused owners toting guns or knives. These break-ins, little smash-and-grab jobs, netted negotiable rings, watches, smokes, and razors. It became routine: scour skuzzy, lipstick-ringed, cockroach- or cigar-dipped glasses, ashtrays fouled by chewing gum, half-eaten mints and candies, and then go out stealthily, early morning, to rattle doors and splinter windows, take whatever was portable and fly, crow-like, to the nearest shadows. He'd return to his snoring rooming house, as quietly as he could, sleep, then rise in the

afternoon to make the rounds with his stolen property, show-
ing up in tavern parking lots to furtively sell his ice-hot razors,
watches, smokes, and rings.

George was overly confident in his crook abilities because of
his proven skill at gambling, another vice he'd acquired in that
assembly of thieves, thugs, rapists, and triggermen otherwise
known as the army. He forgot that a brown-skinned hood,
even if staying out of trouble, is bound to provoke suspicion
from police. But George continued his theft spree blithely.

Then, after three months of success, a Montreal police cruiser
pulled up alongside George, two officers leapt out and, without
even a "bonsoir," frisked him roughly. The constables retrieved,
from the aw-shucks persona of the dishwasher, a jeweller's hammer, a screwdriver, and a flashlight, tools not associated with the
scrubbing of nightclub glasses and not credible for Georgie to
explain in that context. Charged with carrying burglary tools,
George fell into still deeper trouble when a search of his room on
Atwater Street excavated goods impossible for a humble dishwasher to afford, including a $4,000 fur coat, which George
claimed a dancer had given him for safekeeping. It was very
inconvenient for his alibi, however, that the dancer could not be
found because she was, he said, abroad in Egypt.

Unable to prove his innocence, George pulled three months
in jail—one month for the tools, two months for the fur coat—
and went to Bordeaux Prison on the outskirts of Montreal. Bordeaux was not as relaxing as the eponymous wine, but it was
just as ruddy, a boutique, Gothic prison, with massive double
doors as implacable as a drawbridge. To be interred therein was
to vanish from public care, consciousness, and conscience.
George's bed was a mat; his cellmate was a rat as big and toothy
as a dog; his toilet was a bucket; his heating was a radiator that
gurgled and pinged but never felt warmer than an ice cube; his
blanket was a Salvation Army gift but as thin as the pages of

their gift Bible. Still, George enjoyed the Salvation Army troops because they'd speak English with him. The French-speaking guards were really no better than molesters and would deny him food if he couldn't pronounce *J'ai faim* like a French-Canadian. But the Frenchy prisoners were worse. He got beat and pound on, beat and pound on, morning, noon, and night, in the mess hall and in the exercise yard. If he hadn't fashioned himself a blackjack—yard rocks stuck into a sock—he'd've been ground beef for everyone and everyone's blood pudding—what your anus looked like afterwards.

His Majesty's Bordeaux-on-the-Rocks Prison was a news-reel of handcuffs, aspirin, mint-flavoured cough drops, child-size cells of solitary confinement, meals of dry brown bread and cups of green-slime rainwater, sounds of inmates' hacking coughs in the ricocheting metal and tile floors of the freezing nineteenth-century jail, yellow phlegm he brought up way too often, the piss-reek of the cell, roaches gnawing away at law books, the chunky sound of the prison smithy hammering repairs into steel chains and the clanky sound of the cons who had to wear them like perverse jewellery. The dreadfullest sounds was heard in the penal colony on holidays: coughs and cries followed by choking and gurgling. Tears sliding down like falling stars. Suicides by hanging, or by slashing wrists with homemade shivs, razors. Prison made Hell look good.

Commandments were whims: "A bad attitude says you get nothing, or says you get hurt." Any sly inmate was said to be "a chess player with a checkered future."

Under such conditions, George could not even dream of asking Blondola for her hand. All his cash was gone as quickly as it had been won. He wondered how she'd feel about his being a jailbird. He just had to generate some cash.

Once free, George got took on as a chauffeur by the fifty-ish, cadaverous, bow-tied Benny Parole, a man he'd known at

Le Sphinx. Parole had scads and wads of money from his *boîtes de nuit* and his casket-supply business. He had "Georges" drive his several cars to strange destinations to pick up "deliveries." Eventually, Parole sent Georges on a mission where he had to back a new car, its trunk lid open, into a warehouse, to receive a box. Georges felt a heavy weight loaded into the trunk. He drove off, but he was nervous, then heard the sirens behind him before he saw the cops in his rear-view mirror. He swung the car into the alleyway brick side of a building. The trunk top flipped up and George leapt out the car and saw a man's body with a bullet hole in the forehead. Georgie jumped on a train to Halifax—in the dark damp and Haligonian drizzle of April 1946. He scooted and skedaddled southeasterly down to what he prayed would be lucrative alleys, personable alleys, comfy slums.

XIV

I N HALIFAX, the end of the war meant a new, if milder, Depression. The great naval port thrived on war but withered and hibernated between conflicts. Canada's navy, the third-largest on earth, was being scrapped, while soldiers and sailors were turning into students and fathers and relocating to the meccas of Toronto and Montreal, where factory wages could buy washers, televisions, and toasters. So when Georgie tried to find work, there was none for a black boy. Yes, he could shine shoes—again; he could carry bags—again; he could wash dishes—again. But he craved better. He tried to get on Haligonian docks stevedoring, but nothin doin for a Negro—Battle of the Atlantic *he-ro* or not. Nobody wanted his malt, half-Injun face on their payroll. Shit! He'd show up at the Seamen's Union Hall, put his name in for a job, then wait all day, among icy faces and an icy silence, to be called for a task. Everyone else in the hall would be hired to unload one vessel or another, but never George.

Slowly, he began to appreciate that his talents, such as they were, were best suited for wholesome, unquestioning farm labour. In such employ, as at Bezanson's farm, he could work alone, in the open air, savouring smells of wildflowers and blossoms, savouring the feeling of his muscles pitching hay or stooking apples or leading oxen. He enjoyed the powerful honesty of pure labour, agricultural work. But he didn't want to return to Bezanson's barn.

He studied the gigantic map of Canada that covered one wall in the Seamen's Union Hall, squinting especially at the rose-coloured Maritimes. But he'd had enough of Nova Scotia, and he couldn't bear the idea of little flinty, splinter-sized Prince Edward Island. He wouldn't return to Montreal anytime soon either: it was a burgh of cops and jail. He hit on a different future: to ask Blondola to marry him and accompany him to— to Fredericton. It was far enough from Three Mile Plains to suggest they'd moved up in the world but not so far as to make it impossible to visit. George figured he could work as a labourer in the city proper but do small farming outside. Too, he'd have a new life: no one'd know him; he'd know no one.

Now George packed up his suitcase, and caught the train to Windsor. When he saw Blondola again, he could hardly credit her supreme beauty. She had blossomed; she had matured; now an overly pretty sixteen-year-old, the ex-milkmaid had become a darling voluptuous, ripe woman. George was nervous to stand before her in his now patchy army uniform to entice Blondola to come away with him. No letter had gone from him to her in three years, though he had spent months in two prisons and though he had failed to secure serious money.

Yet, from Blondola's point of view, George did look roguishly handsome, and he had been to London and he had seen war; he had seen Buckingham Palace; he had seen the rubble of the House of Commons. He could describe for her places and experiences she had only heard about on the radio. Compared to all her other suitors—the stick-in-the-mud, cowboy-booted bullshitters of Windsor Plains—George was a living cosmopolitan. He even knew a few French phrases (thanks to Bordeaux) and a bit of the Bible (thanks to the Salvation Army). The ex-farm worker, ex-soldier (ex-con) who seemed unafraid of either work or death, who could utter charming, dashing French, and who stood tall in his patched uniform, was certainly more marriageable than the dairy dudes and uncouth drunkards who constituted the other choices. Too, Blondola loved the notion of wedding a veteran.

Polishing his war record and omitting his prison ones, Georgie sweet-talked the impressionable, flattered Blondola into coming with him to see the rest of the world—or at least Fredericton, N.B. That homey town with no Coloured slum. George believed she'd teach him "*terror* don't have half the force of *love*."

Blondola accepted his proposal after a decent interval of hesitation just to heighten Georgie's interest. They married in the African Baptist Church at Three Mile Plains. Rufus was not invited—nor did he attend or send greetings. It was a splendid spring day. Blondola wore a white gown and a crown of apple blossoms. George's army uniform was newly patched and freshly pressed. Blondola's parents gave her away, but neither looked very pleased with her choice of groom. Still, they could brag that George had been to London, even if he hadn't met the King, and he did speak French, though no one around could say how good or bad it was. As for the patches on his uniform, they were forerunners of the medals he would one day truly earn.

The newlyweds boarded a steam train that wept out good-byes to the Annapolis Valley as it cried into Digby. There, they boarded the ferry for Saint John and watched, in the romantic sunset, the boat's white wake turning golden as they left Nova Scotia.

Their marital night was sumptuous. Blondola, sweetly still virgin, wriggled so much it was hard for George to convince her just to clasp him. They were both wet: everything about them—their faces, their chests, their thighs, their sexes—everything was shimmering. They were as wet as newborn infants and practically as pure. George felt new, that he was—they were—blessed. At last.

XV

THE SEAT of York County, situated at the junction of the Saint John River and the Nashwaak River, and bridging both, in the southwest centre of the province, Fredericton, The Celestial City, was ivory drunkenness and false British accents perfected in lumbercamps. It had tried to simulate Boston, Mass., but had ended up emulating Bangor, Maine, a distinct letdown.

Rive sud was mansions, government, elmed and lilac'd streets. But Eatman Avenue, on the north side of the Saint John River, in Barker's Point, was where most Coloureds lived: a place of huts, cops-and-robbers, lumber mills, and railway yards. Here the Ku Klux Klan clucked and conclaved occasionally. The area was named for Lieutenant Thomas Barker, an ex-Yankee and ex-con who landed in 1783 and built a house with iron rings on the walls to hold slaves. From Eatman Avenue, where George and Blondola Hamilton came to dwell, it was common for black boys to stroll with brown girls down to the river to glance at the Gothic and Georgian mansions of the burghers on Waterloo Row and to slingshot stones at the silver-roofed legislature.

But George liked this little city, where his jokes, his labour jobs done cheerfully, and his happy-go-lucky personality seemed to win him neighbourly regard. Also, he was close to the country in Barker's Point, where limited farmland was available. George thought he might come to plant an acre of potatoes, keep a patch for strawberries, and own a couple of maple trees and sixteen hundred bees visiting hundreds of flowers to make honey a salary. He dreamt of one hundred and sixty apple trees, fifty-two fat cows and pigs, to heap up capital in pre-biblical, antediluvian ways. The spot was fertile because of April flooding of the Saint John River, which was thick with trout, salmon, and perch. Here too, on the outskirts of the city, butterflies joshed in assembly, their wings like maps of delight. Geo could enjoy the abundant, soft brains of raspberries. He planned a crop of blueberries and blackberries, also onion, garlic, cucumber, tomatoes, and anything else that could bring the best of Three Mile Plains and Bezanson's Farm back to his nostalgic stomach. He listened to Blondola sing in that shack a man'd sold him for seventy-five dollars. Half-fallen-down, with tarpaper shingles. A small shack with a garden of sorts, a scrawny hen or two.

> *Raspberry wine, sweet, sweet kisses—*
> *You're the well my water misses.*

And they got a reddish cat named Dog.

This outset was a beaut. Blondola loved G. so much, she brought him coffee every morning, in bed. Every morning for how many months—at least six months—she was so much doting on him. And the coffee wafted a lush aroma.

At night, Blondola was a gold seam, a perfumed gold seam. Or she wore Elizabeth of Hollywood's Great Date blouse, in Virgin White—a perfect thrill for her hubby. Blondola said, "Oh, Jawgee, be sweet, sweet, sweet." He could take her like he could take a sip of brandy.

They lived as one, out of a black iron frying pan. It was their wealth, their communion, their experience of time at its fullest.

Blondola asked, "Why shouldn't we be happy? Who don't have molasses, matches, moose meat, and milk?" Why couldn't they enjoy rice and beans, that chapter and verse of the Negro Bible? One day, later, they'd add sausage and lobster.

Weekends they heard saints who played fiddles, angels who played harmonica, and George participated as one of the latter. All those frenzied spiritual tunes were played seraphically, devilishly, by Yours truly, George. Roach would play fiddle and Mrs. Roach would play guitar. And everyone kept time right perfect.

George knew he had to stay out of jail for the sake of his newly bride. If he had to push through suffocating snow to do woods work, to go work on trees, or if he had to ford deep snow to look at traps (and snow always at least a foot deep), there was still love in his gasping and the sweating. When there was money, he paid, with dignification, for a pound of this, a gallon of that.

In early December, George went into the woods to work for a Coloured man, Cy O'Ree, a fortyish oreo with a face like a grave and a smell like a swamp. George felt so unexpectedly blessed. He really wanted to be settled down, a sombre citizen, watch kiddies turn out much better than he had. He was loving to his wife, loving and loving, and he'd give anyone the shirt off his back—if he hadn't already stolen it off their clothesline.

Feelin so uncommonly good, Georgie found out where Rue was floppin in Halifax, then sent him a postcard of Fredericton's Green, with its statue of Robbie Burns, invitin his brother to come on up for a visit sometime. Then he went even deeper into the woods to raise cash for his excellent wife's Christmas.

XVI

EJECTED from Googie's haven and Purity's arms just as the war was ending, in May 1945, Rue drifted. He see-sawed along Halifax's staggered, terraced streets like a standard drunkard. He snooped around, scrounged up gigs. He hung out and gambled. He bobbed up and down the tilting, sliding streets so much, it was a miracle his posture didn't droop. He flopped down nights in boiled-cabbage-dank three-storey wooden boxes girded by three-foot-high weeds.

Times, Rue ducked into cinemas and studied Westerns that always showed the same crises: whisky that burned light like it was kerosene; an indigo locomotive ploughing through horses too slow to evade an obscene liquidation so that their teeth, legs, hooves, bellies exploded into pieces upon the shredding impact; black blood spewing against many white shirts; flies flocking to dead pale mouths; bullets dining, take-out style, on fat guts; smiles shattered by hard fists; the stench of rotten English trapped in a handlebar-moustache. Always satisfying violences. Two shows for ten cents was not too much to ask of Halifax.

Finally, though, Rue'd had all he could stomach of the peace-depressed city. Here there be too much liquor that killed, too much battery acid thrown into jealous eyes. When the King's three-cent postage-stamp face ferried a postcard from Fredericton to Halifax, featuring Georgie babbling about picking French apples and English pears from hundreds of fruit trees, Rue figured there must be pockets ripe for picking in Fredericton.

December 1946. Right after his twenty-first birthday. After barging into Georgie's tiny shack on Eatman Avenue, a replica of The Three Mile Plains abode, Rue eased into tippling backyard concoctions, and smoking, and just feeling evil. Still, he was impressed by the tidy two-room house and trim family Georgie'd concocted. True: George's little home reminded him unpleasantly of the now-incinerated homestead back in Three Mile Plains (it was, for example, cold, drafty, with inconsistent supplies of firewood and food), but it was warm with blankets, kisses, and coffee, and fresh and airy with humming and harmonica. Clearly, Georgie had lucked out. Too, Blondola was such an exasperating beauty that Rufus had to remind himself frequently that she was off-limits, being his sister-in-law. When there was cash in the house, there was beer to drink and homemade pound cake galore—some soft, moist, sweet cake. Amen. Rue could see that Georgie was poor, but. But there was a tinge of joy in that rude household.

Rufus imposed himself on a stove-side, second-hand sofa thrust into the front room. He was prepared to loaf, to eat and drink as haphazardly as fate provided, to plot piano gigs and casual thefts. George made room for Rufus in his tiny house, because they were brothers. But Blondola always cut her eyes at Rue—that grown man who wouldn't work a lick for no one, but just lay about, sucking on a beer or munching on her cake.

Rue sure didn't feel like slavin for anyone: doin Asa-type jobs for stupid, break-ass nothin. That was for Georgie. Instead Rue wandered around Fredton, goin into the Royal Cigar Store at 78 Regent Street to sift through comics, movie magazines, sip a soda. He'd watch the *D. J. Purdy* riverboat arrive one day, then embark for Saint John the next. The city had a few

Coloureds who acted white, would never say "Good day!" They'd turn their heads, cross the street, as if afraid Rue'd brand em with the taint of Africa just by breathin in their direction. The burg was a sight different, with its jail catty-corner to the legislature, and its mansions glaring across the Saint John River at the hovels in Barker's Point. Rudy suspected Fred Town would last forever "cause there's always a need for Hell." For Rue, Fredericton was too suspiciously white to be trusted. He schemed to apply black paint to the statue of Bobby Burns on the Green—either that or smash it to bits.

Passing by the Modernistic Beauty Parlour at 68 Carleton Street, Rufus eyed a beautician stepping down to the sidewalk like Cleopatra disembarking from her glittering barge. She shocked him once because she smiled; then, secondly, because she conjured up Easter. He could've cried when he seen her. Her beauty could destroy pessimism but give optimists something to worry about. Her long, black hair and her big, soft eyes could've belonged to some actress. Her name was India States and she lived near Barker's Point, actually in South Devon, near the South Devon Fuel & Tugboat Company, on Titus (Andronicus) Street, where a small brook perambulated, drunkenly, outside her dusty and muddy shack.

Rue loved watching India's brown hand washfalling through her black, black hair. Truth is, he fell in love with India because of that umber hand and that kohl-coloured hair. Yesss. Rue's hands wished to odyssey through that ocean of black hair. He wanted his and her thighs to slick and click together with body oils. So beautiful as to be Polynesian was India, with her up-to-date wardrobe, her 1947 couture: blouse, skirt, cardigan, black shoes (slight heel), frills, flounces, ruffles. . . . Her ensembles coupled cocoa splendour with rococo accessories.

Rue was quite dreadfully afraid of asking India, whose name

he had yet to learn, to come out with him. But he begged Blon-dola to do him the favour of washing and ironing his best pants and shirt, and then he donned his best Haligonian accent, to style himself as big-city sophisticated. Then he stopped the haughty-seeming beautician on a downtown street to tell her that she was living music who he, as a pianist-composer, had a duty to honour in song.

India just laughed: "Don't tell me you're another Negro jazz player stuck in Fredericton waitin for Duke Ellington to wire you to take the next train to New York." She walked spikily further in her heels, and Rue felt immediately challenged—smitten.

He quickened his pace to stay with her impeccable, sashay-ing form, sunlight turning her skirt filmy, and said, "I don't need no ticket from the Duke for nothin. I'm superior to him." Now India stopped and gave Rue her full attention. He had just enough money, cajoled from Georgie, to ask her to accompany him for a soda.

"A soda? I thought you were a maestro-musician!" India smiled mischievously.

Rue replied suavely, "Seeing as you're a beauty specialist, I need to nourish you with drink that sustains beauty—like tonic water." India was impressed by Rue's vocabulary. She took his arm, and he took her to bed.

India? Her bottom lip stuck out like her bum. Promise of piquant sassiness. Her smell was Ivory soap and Sunlight soap, blended. Would one day they'd share sardines, sausages, bread and butter, crumpets and tarts, and wild blueberries, a break-fast of well-peppered Newfie steak (bologna) and excellent onion soup or burnt-onion hash?

On Christmas Day 1946, India brought Rue some gold sun-flower wine. Her gold dress flared around her like flames. She was pure gold emphatically. Her tongue was Cointreau in his yellow sunflower-wine mouth. Frederictonian sunlight, golden, careened around them in the bittersweet kitchen of a too-short afternoon of groans, rum, prayers, rum, kisses, eggnog, long-ings, nutmeg, kisses, cinnamon, vows, and vanilla. They got into the bathtub together. Rue kissed India—ex-Andalusia, Nova Scotia—right down to her bottom. He didn't want her to glance into the bathwater, fearing she'd—understandably—fall in love only with herself. Her face, in bas-relief, was gold leaf. Honey hair and skin. She had a quarter of black blood, and looked pure gold.

> *You be everythin; lemme call it right:*
> *blue murmurin guitar,*
> *dark rum bruising the throat . . .*
> *Every minute of the day I think of night.*

They were charcoal mellowing blended with soft sugar maple. And India liked Rufus. She felt girded by his strength, and she egged him on to play piano in Fred Town. But not much work for a Coloured man in this city. And Rue refused to humble down. When'd they ever be free to relax and easily *be?*

XVII

DESPERATE for post-Xmas money, Rue shadowed a pimply-faced soda jerk, Omar Bird, into snowy Mazzuca's Lane late at night. Rue snuck up behind Bird and bashed him in the back of the head with a rock. The boy wheezed and slumped down, badly bleeding, but hollering worse. His spectacles had flown free and exploded on the sidewalk. Rue felt the glass shards crunch under his shoes.

He barked, "Shut up!" But a constable, Rex Knox, come runnin, clapped handcuffs on cool, cool Rufus, while Bird sat up, feeling his bleeding scalp and weeping and pointing at the blasé, cigarette-needy man who only felt like smoking, laughing, drinking.

At his trial, Rue charged Knox'd called him a nigger and that he, Rufus James Hamilton, had been trying to help Mr. Bird, who he'd seen hit by another man, who escaped just as Rufus approached. But everyone hated Rue's story.

Rue pointed dramatically at the right side of his head: "I am the real victim of assault here. My bruises be blunt proof." The judge's verdict? "Guilty!" Rue'd go to Dorchester Pen for two years.

The verdict was just a nick to Rue, but it was a knock-out blow to India. She could hardly credit how ridiculous Rue'd turned out to be. Yes, he could dress, he could dress up, and they acted a photogenic pair. Too, Rue had the polish of the boudoir and the poise of the theatre. But in reality he was a pianist who couldn't play piano in any regular style and who couldn't play piano because he didn't have one. To woo her, he had to employ his bumpkin brother's crummy shack. And did he hold any belief for the tomorrow after tomorrow? After Rufus attacked Omar Bird, India felt he'd attacked her and their relationship too. He'd acted like a dumb coward, and she wanted, needed, an intelligent, heroic Negro. Rather than remain in Fredericton and suffer the poison-darted looks of her sister workers and her family, who would shun her for having taken a convicted bungler to her bosom, India collected her wages, her savings from tips, and bought a train ticket for Halifax. She reasoned that if she couldn't land employ as a beautician, she'd join a mortician's enterprise and learn to make the dead look good. She resolved to send Rue no letters. That affair—that love—was now an Ice Age, a prehistory that should be left as blank and fixed as ice. Besides, their union had endured for only a few weeks. Why should she pretend to any loyalty? She was not Mrs. Rufus Hamilton, nor was she his fiancée, nor was she his mistress. She was a singularly glamorous *belle*, one who deserved a courtier of a courter.

The train that delivered Rufus to Dorchester in January 1947 insinuated itself, squirming like an eel, into the muddy sea-like landscape that defines Dorchester, which lays in southwestern New Brunswick, between the Nova Scotia border at Sackville and the Acadian-ruled town of Moncton. When Rue could see around him, he saw a penal-colony building that looked like it'd been sliced off from the Houses of Parliament. Here was the Alcatraz of the Tantramar. Dorchester Penitentiary was like a grand hotel—a Château Frontenac of the bleak marsh. The green-copper-roofed Gothic castle sat islanded on a hill, staring down stark, sawgrass marshes and mudflats caked ochre amid little brittle lances of iced-over blue-black water and a river glistening like oil. Now dusk, it was purple ponds and dark woods. Ice flashed in the never-parched land like a series of broken bones. Crows leapt from carcasses in the wet fields. One was tearing another one apart by the remains of a bridge. Mudflats mirrored a *craquelure* of glazed terracotta, a blood-coloured primeval ooze creased like a crazed brain. Rue'd do his whole stint between January 1947 and December 1948. If he busted out, eluded the snapping dogs and the singing bullets, he'd drown awfully in that abysmal burgundy mud; he'd stand up and get shot down in that mucky, bird-filled, grass-filled no-man's-land.

Inside the medieval-musty prison, its stony enclosures detesting light, was Rufus, being felt up and clubbed and called niggerniggerniggerniggernigger like it was his number and his name. Same treatment struck the other twenty Negro inmates in the harsh pen that held three hundred judge-scolded "wicked" men. The cellhouse's heavy metal doors slammed behind Rue, just as his fist had to slam into other men's faces if he didn't want to be raped. He spied the sun between barbed wire and iron bars for two nasty years in a palace of thugs. Luckily, the con who bunked with him, Octave King, was also niggerish, and bad and black enough not to be messed with. He was in for a pickaxe murder, and he was always known to have a homemade knife around his body, somewhere, and no one wanted to find out exactly where.

Still, Dorchester conjured up Hades. Disgusting insects garnished slop. Inmates made pets of the cockroaches that scuttled over their beds or scraped at crumbs on their lips or clambered down sleeping throats, spurring unfortunate, reflexive vomits that could mean choking to death. Nothing was decent in that prison: not the food, not the soap, not the inmates, not the guards, not the light, not the water. The only fresh air was when cons had to go out into the prison yard, to exercise or to tend to the little farm of potatoes, carrots, lettuce, all of which would be ground down later with mud and served to them as supposed suppers. Of course, there was no piano—busted or otherwise—to think of playing. Rue dreamt hammers hitting strings forcefully. His music was hammer hammer hammer hammer hammer hammer hammer, a stammering thud thud thud thud thud.

Rufus heard of India's defection via hearsay, gossip. She had vamoosed from his life, a wreck, before it could further harm her own. He understood he had lain with a phantasm, an evanescent wisp, one who had taken on flesh and its pleasures for temporary convenience. He shut his eyes and conjured India in his mind, but she was no more real than the contours of India on the prison library's globe. It seemed he had never brushed her lips with his own, never been coddled by her thighs, never heard her laughter in his heart. Her running off to Halifax almost made his blood run cold with sorrow. But, by now, he was accustomed to solo failure and solitary confinement—even outside jail.

XVIII

I N FEBRUARY 1947, after Rue's dispatch to Dorchester, Blondola took pregnant. She and Georgie felt unbelievably prosperous. George just doted on his slender, tender wife. Otho was born in November 1947, and Georgie became Mr. George A. Hamilton, Papa, father of a big, husky baby boy—one born free of any of his convict uncle's criminous habits.

When he brought his wife and baby proudly home to Barker's Point, it was in a taxi driven by cheery Silver, a.k.a. Nacre Pearly Burgundy. He was a short white man, and dapper in his dark limousine, driver-style cap, black wool car coat, and guilelessly courteous, paying clear compliments to Blondola and the baby and being deferential to Georgie. In truth, him and Georgie hit it off right away, because they were both veterans with young families. Silver saluted George as a brother serviceman who was also tryin to improve his self. Silver then showed off snapshots of his own children, while Otho sighed and cooed in his mama's arms.

Right after Otho appeared, George was still doin part-time woodlot work and part-time short-order cook and part-time whatever, and he kept at all these tasks through the lush if ice-flooded spring. In April, Blondola took pregnant again. She sang, Otho fattened and grew, and George just smiled and smiled all through beer-smell summer and crisp, busy autumn.

He never mentioned Rufus; in fact, he forgot all about the "bad man"—as Blondola dubbed him—rusticatin in Dorchester. Nor was there any letter from Rue. Nor was any sent to him.

In December, George elected again to go into the woods to cut timber with O'Ree. He worked even harder than he had in December '46 and December '47, but O'Ree seemed stand-offish, and, times, George saw the auburn man lookin at him ornery. But Georgie just shrugged it off. He figured he'd collect his pay, then hie on home and pick up fresh work in the new year. But when the day dawned, O'Ree tendered no cash.

Instead, him told Georgie, "You's work's poor. Ain't got a cent for you. Scram!"

George saw he'd slaved a whole week for nothin. So Georgie snatched up all the man's tools he could carry, and left.

He got home on Saturday, was arrested for theft on Monday. O'Ree said George was just a thief who ain't done no work. George said O'Ree was lyin, but Georgie had the criminal record. The Laws confiscated all the damned tools—but not a hammer—that Georgie'd lifted. He pulled the same judge as Rue, but fared better: George got a suspended sentence. His efforts to make Cy pay him by taking the tools as collateral on the outstanding debt had backfired and give him a crooked name in Fton. Blondola felt cross and soured on her empty-headed husband. She threatened to go back to Nova Scotia if Joygee didn't smarten up.

XIX

T HEN Rue arrived, with his crooked heart, straight from Dorchester. December 23, 1948. No one happy to see him. And he was grimly unhappy. His brain could still number each single freezing brick of Dorchester—that blizzard of a prison.

Once more Rue sat, grinnin ruthlessly, in Blondola's kitchen, despite all her dirty looks.

His attitude was, "Let a woman weep while a man drinks." She had to be careful, in her own house, not to get too much on Rufus's "nervous nerves." But Blondola was very, very pregnant, and didn't want Rue infectin her Otho with his smell.

She meant every word every time she told Rue, "Go to Hell."

Rue snapped at George, "If Blondola was my wife, she'd keep to her place." George had to let Rufus backtalk Blondola cause the army hadn't made George as muscular as jail had made Rufus, and he'd exited the pen in a bad mood. But George's pacifism worsened Blondola's anger.

Christmas 1948 was hardly Christmas. Little cheer in the Hamilton camp (as a judge would later call the house). And there was a hammer on the premises, but no piano.

As for India, she'd fallen for a dandy, fancy talker in North End Halifax, a sporting ladykiller who'd proven another vapid con. However, she saw his emptiness and saw through his vaporous promises only after he had bade her womb welcome a lifelong customer for her beautician's art and a fervent worshipper of her taperings and curves. She'd not married her Lucifer—despite his charms—but she had settled all her love upon her child, her daughter, while relegating men, Negroes especially, to the outer limits of untouchability: they were smooth in speech, slick in bed, but too slippery to hold.

India became a beautician at the Canadiana Hair Salon in downtown Halifax. She took up residence in the room above, with her lipsticks, her perfumes, and her babe in arms. She became adept at fashioning "Canadian" hairstyles—all derived from Montreal. Her customers left the salon looking like film stars, but always ended up with ruffians who looked like they had just left a saloon—because they had. Nevertheless, by looking good, the women felt better about their bad choices. This cosmetic salvation also applied to India herself.

XX

BY JANUARY 7, 1949,
Asa was disappeared in Halifax;
Cynthy was buried in Windsor;
Easter was drowned in the Avon River;

Reverend Dixon was kicked destroyingly in his side by a horse;

Googie and Purity was jailed cause bawdy houses were "a Communist plot";

India was a lone parent, toiling as a beautician in Halifax;

Blondola was fresh in the hospital;

George was free, but broke;

Rue was broke, but free.

Morning: snow sifted over two mourning, superficially smooth mugs. An ashen omen of snow: too much like two cold boyhoods in Three Mile Plains. It fell like dry and cold flakes of ash.

On January 7, 1949, there was no money and no food and wood in the house. No rabbits hung from roof beams; no deer carcasses dangled in a shed.

On January 7, 1949, twenty-two-year-old Rue felt as bad as alcoholics with that violent craving. He was as desperate as them drunks who attack each other, tearing open each other's bowels and stomachs, hoping that drinking each other's blood'll give em the alcohol they crave. He felt his whole life—his future too—

depended on moolah and a lick or two of rum—Pusser's Navy rum, please.

On January 7, 1949, in that shack on Fredericton's edge, twenty-three-year-old George Hamilton was a father twice over, with Blondola closeted in the hospital downtown with the latest, and without money. Hear Dog, the rusty-coloured cat, meowing crazily with hunger.

The brothers was once scrawny, beaten-up black boys. Now, they was thin black men, with black, angular caps and second-hand denim shirts. They was needing so much, beginning with love and respect and ending with beer and cash. They'd have to clip a jerk and swipe his budget. If they had the spunk. If they had such verve, Rue'd extract new clothes now trapped in the cleaners and go to Halifax to rescue India, and Georgie'd retrieve a wife and newborn child now immured in the hospital.

To snitch and snatch was the answer to *empty* and *used-up*. The air was cold in that shack: words could practically be traced in the white mist that cracked their mouths. Not even their blood flowed right in this winter. They had to burn wood—or freeze. All-important kindling dwindled. They was in a jam.

"The universe is perfect," thought George, "except for us."

Their breakfast did not include fogging oatmeal in a white china bowl anointed with Quebec maple syrup and cream, or butter slathered over gold cornbread, or yellow eggs, pink ham, and green-white onion sighing in the black Eden of an iron frying pan. They did not consume honey and oranges either. Not even no salt pork and brown biscuit—as in the days of the first Hamiltons a sesquicentennial back. The current Hamiltons had only the benediction of hot coffee. (Rue cussed: "Shit! Make it dark black!")

If they could've starved the hungriness out their bellies, they would've. Their day offered no church of holy warmth, no salvation from the hellish cold. There was no Wharf Sale of cold plates, baked goods, produce, or tea. (They couldn't've bought anything, anyway.) They had a trickle of smoke to keep from freezing. (Fire split the stove: half wood, half flame.) Clothing was no help. They couldn't sheathe themselves in cotton undershirts, or wool pullovers. Nor were there lambswool coats or leather gloves and boots.

Rue averred authoritatively, "I'm so hungry, not even wolves could scare me off a meal."

George commented, "Why doncha get a job? Bring some loot into the house."

Rue glared coldly. "You think we gonna redcap? Shit! We's gonna stay slaves forever!" He paused, then snapped: "Somebody want to shovel shit on us? Well, we'll shovel it right back." Rue had philosophy: "Joygee, ya gonna go on biggin up Blondola every year, letting her shit out babies year after year, bang, bang, bang, with nothin in the bank?"

George just looked at his frozen-faced brother.

"Ya wanna have children, Joyge, ya gotta have cash. Look at what poverty did for us! Nothin!"

George replied: "I been working honest to provide for the wife and house."

Rue guffawed: "Joygee, we is just thieves, pure thieves. We steal firewood, chickens, clothes off clotheslines, even fools' bad ideas."

George's rejoinder: "Sin's on ya like lice, Rudy."

Rue just smiled. "All I'm sayin is, we stun and rob a man. I ain't sayin he gotta be hit hard enough to kill."

In his mind's eye now, George saw a white man staggering, bloody and wallet-less, through a downtown alley, maybe Mazzuca's Lane.

The decision to go out and hit a white man real hard to get some cold cash did not require much dialogue:

George: You was sayin…
Rue: You know what I mean…
George: That right there.
Rue: It's like that.

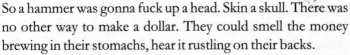

So a hammer was gonna fuck up a head. Skin a skull. There was no other way to make a dollar. They could smell the money brewing in their stomachs, hear it rustling on their backs.

But there was contentiousness. Otho—thirteen months old—ate at Mrs. Roach's house cause there was no food in his own, and his mama was confined with his newborn sister, Desiah, cause Doc Clayton Pond's delivery bill was unsettled. Georgie couldn't just go back in the woods and hammer down some trees, because he had to baby Otho. He couldn't leave Otho with Mrs. Roach every day cause she had three children of her own. Mr. G. Hamilton'd already been to the Unemployment Office in downtown Fredericton. But there was no porter job on the train, no white man hirin help, no company wantin two arms to lift, shift, and steady packages. Worse, he couldn't hoist a beer because he didn't have none: when your pocket's dry, your mouth's dry.

George left Rue dreamin at the kitchen table in the afternoon and took a bus downtown and visited Blondola at the Fredericton General Hospital. She was lookin good, feelin better. George'd hardly peeped at his daughter, Desiah, when crippled up, white-haired Doc Pond, wobbling on his crutches, called him out into the corridor and said, "Georgie, we're gonna keep your wife and baby here until you pay my bill or give me a welfare slip from city council." Georgie didn't go back in the hospital room, but faced the chilly Friday, January 7th air of 1949, and caught the bus at King and Westmoreland.

He got him home at about 4 p.m. Where Rue was, he hadn't a

clue. His feet and hands were so cold he could hardly coax fire out the matches and the couple sticks of wood he'd boosted in the neighbourhood. Then, he tidied the embarrassingly barren table and trudged over to Mrs. Roach's to pick up Otho. When Georgie entered the Roaches' place, he was surprised—and not—to see Rue, sittin at Mrs. Roach's big maple table, finishin up a steamin plate of beans and wieners. Weren't Rue evil enough to reach for a pitcher of maple syrup and pour a gallon of it, slowly, cruelly, over that hot, fulfilling food, but to do it casually too, as if it were not a feast? Rue smiled, then took Mrs. Roach's delicious homemade brown bread, dipped it in molasses, scooped up some beans, and ate like a king. Unfair: him could solicit anything out of anybody, but here was Georgie, starvin.

A fortyish, cedar-skinned, big, amiable woman, Mrs. Roach didn't offer George food, but she let him sit by the stove for warmth, then she went into a bedroom to get Otho. George ask Rue what he'd done all day.

Rue snapped, "Slep."

George say, "Why doncha help put sumpin into the house?"

Rufus, coldly: "I's no slave."

Mrs. Roach come back, hand goo-gooing Otho to Georgie, ask, "Why doncha play sweet on your harmonica, Joygee?" George obliged. He played his Dante Marine Band harmonica, dirty, frothily, as if he were on stage at the Capitol Theatre in Saint John, and Mrs. Roach grinned and patted her hefty thighs in rhythm. He blew out the blues songs that he'd perfected on the high seas during the war: "Burning Water" and "Death Be Gentle." (Those hungry for true blues remembered George Hamilton was always anxious to please.) But Georgie was too shy and too ashamed to beg Mrs. Roach for biscuits and beans.

The brothers lingered at Madame Roach's abode until her man, Roach, trudged in from the woods, at about 5 p.m., along with Jehial States, who was so crafty as to seem a simpleton, but was actually so astute as to work only when he wished and to do his best work when he was least sober. Roach, a fiftyish lumberman, plaid-shirted, plaid-jacketed, blue-jeaned, and workbooted, with a stocking cap on and brown plug tobacco and a black pipe in a pocket, him had a bottle of red wine and a dozen tall beer he set generously on the table. Then they all got busy—except the missus and the children—sipping wine and tippling beer and blaring blues to harmonica. But one man was hungry and another was angry.

The boys got wine and beer from Roach, to settle their blasphemated guts. By 7 p.m., Roach swayed so elegantly—blind drunk, he seemed to float out his front door, but pissing himself as he went.

George—cradling a squalling Otho—and Rufus returned to the redoubt of Master George A. Hamilton, Esquire. Frankly hard up, they parleyed about their zilch cash.

George had a suggestion: "Break into a store, a house, a car, lift some goods." Anything solid turns liquid in crooked hands.

Rue hissed, "That's no good, we want cash." The correcto idea was, as Rufus'd hinted that morning, to go to Fton, pick a man, pull him in an alley, knock his noodle to his ass, haul his wallet out his pocket, scram.

George blurted, "I don't wanna go to Dorchester for two years!"

Rue rejected that riposte: "I had fucked-up luck two years ago. I ain't wouldn't've even had to go out that night if you'd had a drop of drink in this house for your brother. It's only a little bitty job to slug a sucker." Besides, Rue wanted "a fur cap, a fur coat, and a silver-handled, silver-tipped walking stick, please and thank you."

George: "Okay, but ya need a blackjack." George got his poverty-struck toolbox, and the boys rummaged its paltry, poor-condition contents until Rue, recalling a piano, picked out a hammer. George whistled: the hammer could work.

Then, hulking, horse-faced Plumsy Peters knocked to see what the boys had to drink. Rue drawled his answer, "Naw, but we's gonna get some—if you mind the house, keep the fire goin." George added: "And keep an eye to Otho." Plumsy nodded okey-dokey. Slow-witted, with a bumpy face, he could cook and steal: his skills kept him in food and clothes, if not in lodging and drink.

Roughly 7:30 p.m., the Hamiltons walked down Eatman Avenue to the Richibucto Road: two dark men tossing shadows like knives into the unsuspecting white snow. They passed the Roaches, said "Good night." Then Rue approach Roach, ask him to "hold on to" a lighter. Roach give him two dollars for the pawn, then Rufus run back up to where George was. Good fresh cash for a beer and the bus. It come, they got on, sat at the back by two gals they knew—Yamila James and Zelda King. The bus rattled, wheezed, left the duo at Carlton and Queen streets, smack dab in Fred Town. From here, they could not go wrong. But that hammer stuck in Georgie's back pocket, it didn't hang right.

They passed a billboard pledging "Jesus Saves" and another billboard, by a nearby grocery, swearing "Swanson saves you more." Hungry—hungry, Geo thought: "Only water in my stomach." Rue was cold-blooded cold. Blown from roofs, snow the shade of pure milk—or impure night—snuck down with the lacy, sure manoeuvres of a million generations of spiders. They tromped past the legislature; it sat near Fredtown's mansioned riverfront strip, Waterloo Row. From here, the boys could look across the river to the shacks of Barker's Point. The moon: an albino slug breathing against a black-soil sky.

Rue breathed out a cold mist to tell George to hit and lug a fool into an alley. But it was Friday night.

"Too many people on the street. No way to hit a man."

So George said, "I'll phone a taxi." He took out his wallet, empty cept for three cab company cards, and chose Elroy's Taxi. He stepped into a phone booth and dialled. A woman answered; a taxi'd pick em up outside the Canadian Legion hall in ten minutes. Georgie said as much to Rue, who decided to go into the Legion to buy a beer. He come out a couple minutes later without a beer.

Rue say, "Joygee, those people is crazy in there. They won't sell me a beer without a membership." Nothing to do, then, but choose who'd clip the driver. Rufus resolved: "Joyge, it's your plan, your hammer, and you're the one carryin it."

George nodded.

It were a foolproof plot, yep. But designed by one fool and one foolhardy *philosophe*.

Then the cab arrived and George shook. He was expecting a stranger. But here was Silver—leaping to open the passenger side doors of the black Ford sedan with black leather upholstery for George and Rufus as if they was gentlemen. Silver wore a black sable coat, black leather shoes, a black-looking cap, and his usual warm, azure eyes.

HAMMER

*My truth is a hammer
coming from the back.*

—THULANI DAVIS, *X*

I

WHEN Rue saw Silver, he saw red. He saw a man with an invisible X marked on the back side of the right side of his skull. Like on a treasure map. Maybe Silver's wallet was pregnant with a small fortune in small bills. And the hammer was frankly iron, steely in its certainty, and it could bang up silver.

Rue slid in front, George in back.

Silver settled back, asked, "Where to, Georgie?" George directed Burgundy, who he'd known for three and a half years, out to the Wilsey Road: a perfect place for wielding a hammer violently, in peace.

Rue was just as cash-famished. Rue was desperate to get his good winter clothes out the cleaners. He had, oh, bout eight dollars' worth of *habiliments* stuck fast there. Rue was too dapper to wear borrowed, raggedy "Georgian" overalls forever. As suave as a pulp villain, he was a black knife thrusting into a penal landscape of white. He was an ebony piano key sharply out of key with the surrounding ivory ones. He craved big money in coin and paper, and bullion, not bullshit.

Face the facts: cold'd left the two lads uncomfortable and shit out of luck. Winter was leaning mean, loud, and bitchy against the walls of their drafty castle. It stank of hunger. The boys'd hunker by some fossil of a fire, its flames shivering worse than they was. Ice in their bathwater now injected itself into their blood. It was so cold, it was blissfully warmer to trudge through snow, to push through snow, to move face-first into blazing cold amid pieces of scattering woods.

The brothers—raw, black moderns—and their driver, sil-very, swung past the Harvard-styled red-bricked University of New Brunswick, its terraced and treed slope overlooking the south bank of the Saint John River. They passed factories churning out shoes, soap, canoes, toothpicks, toilet tissue, and candy, but not hiring any Negroes.

The boys advised their driver to wheel the snowed-on, obscure hillbilly routes, ostensibly in search of a bootlegger who'd sell em hooch. But the hammer was there, in Georgie's back pocket, a freezing, constant erection he couldn't just sit on. Georgie looked out frosty windows at the snow-dirtied, snow-blasted roads, the pines as black and thick as mourners lined up almost onto the road itself, damn near close, and his gloveless hands barely warm in his pockets. Rufus bandied words with Silver, waiting for Georgie to strike from behind, when he, Rufus, would deliver a stunning punch. He's hooting, grimacing, teeheeing, but waiting for that opportune split sec-ond when, after a little bloodshed, just a little, the hard-working taxi man's stash will be his—and partly Georgie's—to spend on what they want: booze, yes; cootchies, yes; a dashing silk suit, yes (if the cash don't run dry).

But George had second thoughts even as the taxi bill rose higher every second. After all, Silver'd driven his first baby home from the hospital, delivering wife and newborn as kindly as a doctor. Maybe more so. Still, the carpentry hammer shifted awkwardly, rigidly, but nigh imperceptibly in the right back pocket of Georgie's overalls. He was no paragon of cogitation, but he didn't need to be. No, he be just hungry for warmth, starving for firewood, and also needy for scratch for beer, some silver for a slice of blueberry pie and a Coke, maybe precious silky black stockings for Blondola.

They got to Dibs Cromwell's place on Wilsey Road, and Georgie jumped out cause he knew he couldn't hit Silver. He had to shake off the fear. Feelin cold'd help. Georgie played off like he was serious about visiting Dibs, but he only went halfway up to the house, then returned. Rufus eyed George's vague intentions intently. Silver calculated how much Georgie already owed him and how much tonight would up the tab.

Georgie returned and Silver ask, "Where to next?"

Georgie could feel Rufus's icy disgust, but said, "Over the river, to Ken Morris's, his house is diangle to Cromwell's." The trio motored back across Fredericton to Barker's Point, near Eatman Avenue, to go by Morris's place. This time, Silver stopped in front of Morris's house cause he was havin doubts about what Georgie was doin.

Well, George stepped out, knocked, and when Morris answered, George asked, sheepish, "Ken, you know where Dibs Cromwell is?"

Morris: "Nope. Go way, Georgie."

Rue had the will to stamp on Silver. The Boston Tailors shop downtown was selling New English and Scots Wool Gabardine Ladies' Suits and Men's Suits. Silver could furnish Rue with a winter wardrobe.

"Hittin Silver will be just like blowin my nose—cept much easier," he thought. The snow glared affirmatively. But Georgie had the hammer.

Clambering again into the rear of the cab, George felt relieved. There'd be no hittin Silver tonight. Time to go home.

Silver said, "Where to this time, George?"

George said, "Home."

Rufus coughed. "Where'd you say we was goin, Georgie?"

George said, "Home."

Rue turned to Silver. "Naw. Silver, run us up to Jehial's."
Silver was tired of this backing and forthing. He guessed the
brothers wanted bootleg.

"Boys, want to split a beer? I got nice cold ones in the trunk."
He'd take them up to Jehial's and sell them ale too: only sixty
cents a bottle.

Rufus smiled: "Sure."

Georgie couldn't think. The Ford blasted through the snow-
bound, starry night.

Silver don't mind selling booze out his trunk, and he don't
need payment up front since, because he owns two of the four
taxis in all of Fredericton, a thirsty pedestrian has got to come
calling on him again. In the meantime, the interest on their beer
purchase and ride may have escalated prettily.

Silver's a good man among very few good men, a veteran of
the Hitler War who came back, delivered milk, got hitched,
bought a house, then got into the taxi business, buying two cars
and paying a second driver. His wife—petite, sweetheart
Donna—was the dispatcher. She'd taken the call that set him
out on this hours-long bootleg quest. Problem was, nobody'd
pour a pint or a teaspoon for these two Coloured chaps who
were always out of pocket, always wastrels, and who were
dumbfounding at sports, but, otherwise, were undependable
lazy asses, once intoxicated.

As Silver saw it, the centuries-misplaced and ocean-displaced
Negroes, stranded in New Brunswick since 1783, had a problem with *Civilization*, its culture of taxes and jails, for they dared
to love *Freedom* too much, liquor and lovin too much, music and
guffaws too much, and were ornery, contrary, and disrespectful.
They was natchally uppity, sassy, seditious, loud. They made
poetry only when making fists—or making love.

Fair to say, Silver felt no malice toward em; they were, he
mused, as God had shaped em, and there was nothing white

to be done about it. They seemed to like the squalor and the shacks and the shitty work. They quit early on schools, bought junk, ate maggoty meat, and begged to haul garbage, mop up other people's filth and vomit, or do witless jobs: shovelling snow, laying down tar, whatever it took that didn't take brains. Often surly, they'd laugh explosively, blaring white teeth for an instant, then retreat into silence. Like chillun, they lived off this and on that. True, Silver regretted slavery, too bad it happened. He don't think his ancestors were involved in that grotty trade. But even if they had been, so was everybody else. His duty was to ferry Negroes, on credit, to the bank (rarely), the grocery store (weekly), bootleggers (nightly). He wished em well, and he wished the Hamilton boys would settle on a destination. But that Georgie could whistle and manhandle harmonica classically, and his brother, "Rupe" or something like that, was fun—a frothing Atlantic of stories. But tonight, Georgie's harmonica harmonized nothing. The pristine four-door Ford sedan hummed on, blackly, into the snowy, moonlit woods.

Georgie was already tastin them "bews"—as he spoke it—in his head. He were happy to place the beverage on the taxi bill. George was thinkin he'd just tell Silver he'd square up next week. On that score, Rufus was ever more visibly agitated. The plan he'd agreed on with Georgie wasn't bein executed. No: profits were bein pissed away in beer and turned into a Sargasso of debt. He saw red. Him wanted blood, then red wine, then pussy, then his pressed pants. In that easy order. Why waste words, time, budget on drinkin some white boy's price-hiked beer and tourin the boonies of a nowhere province in the freezing-ass winter, when you could just tap the sucker on the skull, jack his dough, commandeer his car, buy tall beer, and claim a sugary dame? There's no question in Rue's head about what this gab and fabrications predicted. But Georgie had the hammer, so him should do the clippin. Rue's lust to hear a man holler was bad enough to make himself want to holler. He peered hungrily at the side of Silver's head, but couldn't hardly see through the dark.

The sedan slid icily to a stop at the bottom of Poplar—or Popple's—Hill, just off the Richibucto Road, in the driveway of Jehial States, a couple miles north of Eatman Avenue where the boys lived. It slid. To a stop. Everyone lurched forward, shifting from half-in-shadow to half-in-moonlight and back again. Blurring.

Neither bothered nor pleased, Silver whistled and, because Jehial's house was on a slight slope, turned the car around so it was aimed at the legislature across the river. Fredericton's lights sparkled through the winter night, competing with the stars, across the frozen-up Saint John.

The moon glowers. Silver, Rufus, and George exit the car: slick black in moonlight, sleek black against snow. Their feet go *crump*, *crump* through the squeaky snow. Their breaths are pale, ephemeral amoeba. Silver whistles "Auld Lang Syne"; he goes to the trunk.

George walks with a loping slouch. He'd shifted the hammer from his back pocket to the inside of his shirt, and, as he'd left the car, it'd fallen out, luckily, into plush snow. Silver, not lucky, got out the opposite side, missing the hammer.

He cracked the trunk: "How about that bottle of beer?"

George: "Okay!" He sweated inside his seemingly ice-cold blood and nerves, almost delirious that, by losing the hammer, he'd prevented further damnation.

The radio bleated hits tearful, excited. "Route 66," "Nature Boy," "Lush Life." The light jangle of change in Silver's pocket chimed with the "moon-spoon-June" jingles. The coins shifting in Silver's pocket sounded to Rue a lot like jailer's keys. He shuddered. No one paid any mind. But the noise was proof of piles of cash on Silver. Rue could imagine Silver as a Royal Bank manager, flush with money flashing George VI's mocking face. Smell of woodsmoke pungently, sight of blue smoke shifting erratically in air, taste of runny noses on upper lips. Silver opened the trunk, got the boys one beer to share. The trio did get nicely on in ale. But if anyone fell down drunk, there was a blanket in back of the car.

The stars were flint, just broken bits of light, there, on the Richibucto Road, right outside the city limits and right beside obsidian wilderness. No better spot, amen, to use a hammer. Moonlit, the wind blew cold. The moon could tree and hang itself forever. The woods they'd stopped by was chilly but welcoming. Sleep couldn't be too far. After sharing a beer, after waking a bootlegger. In the meantime, everyone's shivering; six hands shaking with the tall brown New Brunswick beer bottle as it goes around.

As Silver lowered his hand, the moonlight shot off the pretty chrome casing of his Rolex Victory watch, a souvenir for war vets. Brown leather bound the timepiece to Silver's wrist, its skin as fragile as that of a butterfly. At Silver's neck, a black glass-bead rosary flashed. Silver was a slight, short man. He could be eclipsed. He could be taken without too much force. Here was a modus operandi, more or less. Rufus glared at Georgie, said nothing.

He thought, "Don't Silver look a lick like Elmer Fudd?"

Far as Rue was concerned, Georgie was fuckin up again. And all he had to do was bust out Silver's brains. He was, as usual, the rough part of a smooth plan: Would George hit Silver, please, so they could go into a house and eat?

Rue said to George, "Let's go off a ways to chat about that gal."

Silver laughs: "Can't a married man listen in?"

Rue says, "You'll hear all bout it later." He puts an arm around George and they huddle away some paces from the car. White breath and black words venting.

Georgie was feelin queasy. "Well, I dropped the hammer."

Rudy ask, "Where?"

George said, "Other side of the car."

Frowning disgust, Rufus now ask, "What's wrong wit ja, Joygee? Lost yer nerve?"

George say, "Ain't hittin Silver. He's been a pal."

Rufus was unmoved: "Huh. Yer yellow skin's yellow from the bone."

George whimpered, "You want me to knock im off?"

Rue say, "You ain't gonna hit him, I gonna hit him. Smack the fuck outta him."

George almost sobbed: "Jiminy Cripes! No!"

Now Rue was just disgusted. "Damn it all to Hell!"

George protest: "I can't hit Silver. I knows him."

Rufus affirmed, "I gettin some cash money, get ma clothes out the cleaners. That's that."

George stamp his feet and shuffle a bit. "Why don't we just knock over the damned cleaners?"

Rue'd not equivocate: "We'll split the take dollar for dollar. We'll sit at the big table, counting out his money."

Jittery, George yelled over to where Silver was standin, "Silver, you know any cathouses round here?"

Silver let out a big laugh: "Beer's gettin cold!"

The Hamiltons drifted back to the car. As they approached the vehicle, and while Silver's vision was still blocked by the open trunk and while George was musing about the moonlight, Rue noticed where the hammer lay, only slightly shrouded by snow, and figured he could retrieve it, if-when needed, without much notice. Silver say, "Cheers, boys!" The bottle circled in the brilliant dark, followed by slurps. An opera of fraternity.

The car radio crooned saxophone and tambourine; it was the gravelly crooning of Nat King Cole striking sparks off ice. Cigarette-black and brackish phlegm spat into snow. Issuing from beer-oiled throats, men's cussings mixed together Prime Minister Saint-Laurent and shit. But nobody noticed how evil multiplies, fanning out and circulating like the money supply—M1—itself.

The radio spoke a newspaper sermon. Men in black leather shoes and white cotton shirts and sable silk ties were about to decide the future. Mao was driving white moneybags out of China, but the Brits and the Yanks wanted to make him stop. Hollywood beauties were posing just as, elsewhere, nationalist Chinese and their allies were fleeing. The Royal Bank was bulking up on broken treaties and buffalo bones.

The New Brunswick government announced, "The battle against venereal diseases is being fought relentlessly. A Division of Dental Health has been added…."

Silver screeched at the idea of dentists checking crotches. The Hamiltons howled louder.

Silver ask, "Boys, guess what this province's first-ever law was?" George and Rufus look at each other, shrug. Silver say, "A law to outlaw fucking sheep!"

The guys giggled. But what if the sheep liked being fucked by farm boys?

Silver opened up his wallet and, as the dreamy, glossy bills flickered in the moonlight, paraded photographs of his blond darling children, his stunning looker of a wife, Donna, glistening, sleek. She was the tenderly looked-after kind of blonde who could expect to sport a new mink coat every Christmas. Georgie gulped the acid of envy; Rufus smiled glaringly, extra brittle. Fragments of hard snow, spiking down, nailed loneliness into Rue's heart, with early January of 1949 falling into history, with night and with chill, but without solace.

Silver sipped and mentally added up his bill, while standing in the snow looking at a cackling Rufus and George.

He wondered, "Are they ludicrous, or are they stupid?" See George, his cigarette drooling with his words because his nerves now made him feel small, shitty, and awkward. See Rue, looking like a jolly golliwog.

"Some can't handle booze, and others won't," mused Silver. He had a sudden taste for red-and-white wine—the colour of blood on snow. The 1949 Custom Model Ford sedan glowed hotly in the cold.

Three men were there, drinking a single bottle of beer, together, before midnight. Just three men glad to be alive on a frigid night.

There were no complaints. No diagnosis of brain damage or lesions. No immeasurably deep snow. No mudflats adjacent, not really. No bloody blanket. No charred crucifix. No easy road to Saint John or to Hell. No dark rum. No tears. No host of crows. No talk of Robbie Burns's statue, snow-topped, on the Green in Fredtown, its back turned against the river and scowling up at the university. No rills of meltwater cascading in a gully. No one laid low against the law. No blue-eyed nihilism. No well-dressed surliness. No complaints.

II

GEORGIE announced he'd stop up at Jehial's, that rough, brown-moon-faced man, since they was parked in his driveway. Just go knock on the door and see if there was home brew about. Nice if some beer'd come in, or a quart of rum.

Adjusting his dark-coloured taxi cap, Silver crooned, "Fine, fine." All was fine.

Georgie trudged up the ice-slick, hilly path. Rue and Silver shrank under the blackening moonlight and their chuckles and chat grew subtler the further George rose up that hill and neared Jehial's door. He banged on it four, five times.

He hollered; then Jehial hollered, "Who there?"

"George Hamilton."

Jehial said, "Show your face so I can see you." George stood at the flimsy deal door.

Him ask, "You got any home brew?"

Jehial spoke through thin pine. "Aincha drunk nough tonight? I know I has."

George parried: "Blondola an me just got a new baby girl."

Unseen, Rue slipped into the front seat of the car beside the slightly tipsy Silver. He was almost unheard.

(The wind bears the sound of a man crying "Oh!")

Jehial ask, "What was that? Ya creep up here to thief my kindling?"

George protested: "When Blondola comes out the hospital, come on down and have dinner with us."

III

A HAMMER'D hit Silver like a train. His ears—once ringing with music and laughter—were now ringed with blood. A detonation of blood inside the car: a deafening roar inside Silver's skull. His head slumped on his neck and spewed red ooze. Moseying blood slid down.

Imagine the blood aquariuming Silver's brain. The resistless hammer squashing the egg of the brain, its lobster-paste *merde*, its waspish humming. Then a dynamite of pain. Imagine the whiplash of the hammer, the sizzle of it against the skull, the brilliant cum of blood, accumulating redness, almost like a cloud, and the *sussurus* of pain, molesting, eclipsing, his nerves. The whinnying blood. Silver's last breaths making a noise like hardwood cracking. To make his skull a bloody egg, smashed open like a *piñata*, consciousness seeping out, sparkling.

The hammer bit into and took away a cleft of ear too, like a hungry dog dragging down a pig. The hammer thudded against the skull with the same lasting tone of piano hammers striking strings. Its solid and sucking ingress brought on an egress of liquids and sighs. Silver was expectorating blood onto the steering wheel and the back of the front seat.

After five minutes at Jehial's, George said, "See ya!" He clambered carefully down the tricky driveway, and went to Silver's taxi from the back.

From the right side of Silver, Rue bark, "George, take the wheel."

George went straight to the front of the car and looked in. He saw Silver. His head lay back over the front seat. Georgie then snapped open the driver-side door, ask, in a muffled shout, "What happened here?"

Rufus cussed, "You lost your nerve so I hit the so-and-so cause I ain't goin home without cash to get my coat out the tailors and my clothes out the cleaners."

George whimpered: "You shouldn't've done it! I told ya I know the man."

Rue snarled: "I's gettin cash and my clothes out the cleaners.'"

Rue pulled the wallet out Silver's back pocket, and stuck it, grinning, in his own shirt pocket. Rue caressed the snoozing man's wallet, enjoying its smooth and still-body-warm feel. He felt uplifted. He giggled involuntarily, nervously, in homage to his sense of relief and of joyous accomplishment.

George doubled over, not to laugh but to vomit, though nothing would come. He say, "Why doncha smooth over Silver's hair, hide that big injury in his head?"

Rue snorted: "Quit fumbling, Jawgee! Strip off his watch—it looks like gold—and that silly black rope around his neck. Take his wedding ring too."

George got to work. He tore his buddy's Rolex Victory off the limp left wrist. It felt like cool bone in his hands. Rue thrust his fist insolently down Silver's right pocket and withdrew a handful of silver and some paper money. Georgie did the same on Silver's left and got silver off the pocket. Grunting, George tugged the wedding ring of hammered gold off Silver's hand and stuck it in his own pocket.

Rue said, "Silver's just a little bit fucked up, I guess."

"What we gonna do?"

"Drive." An awful lot of blood rinsed on him.

Georgie shoved Silver's short form aside with his hips as he took the wheel. He was now the proud owner of a mint-condition—if soiled—1949 Ford. Rue sat on Silver's right. Two erect bodies kept slumping Silver's body propped upright. George donned Silver's navy blue taxi-driver's cap, now violet. Boots went squelch, squish, squelch on the carpeted floor of the car, already whorishly wet.

First they drove without lights because George couldn't master the headlights. He fiddled desperately with all the dashboard switches and knobs. He drove Silver and his brother—as if they were picnicking—down to the Lyric gravel pit back of the Hamilton shack on Eatman Avenue. They had to navigate snowy roads so strewn with potholes, any new car would look raggedy, old, and beat up after only a few miles. Parked invisibly in the gravel pit, now argentine as a moon crater, the boys completed their cannibalizing of Silver's property.

George riffled through the wallet, divvying up the hard-to-come-by, dollar for dollar. Twenties, tens, fives, twos, and ones. Silver sat there in the silvery light and nodded his acquiescence. George got $88 and the watch and the ring; Rufus had $87 but also grabbed the clutch of coins. He also unhooked Silver's black glass crucifix and beads.

The fraternal assailants stumbled from that snowy black car, its driver's seat ruddy as if in a state of ruins. There be bloodstains on the rear left door of the sedan as well as a black streak on the upholstery behind the driver's front seat, and then further incrimination, crimson, dripping onto the rear right door on the metal trimming. Bleeding turned the snow slushy silvery pink.

Rue now detailed a plan to stuff Silver in the trunk and deposit cab and cabby on a wharf in harlot-and-what-have-you Saint John, so cops'd pin this battery on the loose citizens of that *louche* city. But George said nope, leave Silver on the side of a deserted road. Rufus shrugged.

The lads drove six or seven miles down the opaque Richibucto Road, swerved into a half-forgotten by-road, then slid down a slope and, thus, smack into the frame of an abandoned, rotting car. This accident busted the right-hand parking light of the Ford and scraped it up. Georgie backed up six or seven feet. Then he got a blanket from the trunk and laid it on the black snow. Rue and him hauled Silver from the car. They was gonna dump Silver in any old snow under a tree. George had his shoulders, Rue had his feet. Unbuttoned, Silver's head looked bad. The wound in his head was prettier than a scab, lovelier than a scar would have been.

Rufus guffawed, "He look fly-ugly." He laughed. "Nope, he be fly-on-a-pig-ugly."

George joked: "He look fly-on-a-pig-in-shit-ugly." Now gut-splitting laughter—to the edge of tears.

Rue say, "He is shit-ugly!"

George still had a mood to screech as they took the soft, yielding Silver and laid him onto the blanket, wrapped him up, then carried him six yards in the woods and stretched him beneath a pine, on government snow, upon Crown land.

In the car, George found a flashlight under the dashboard. He turned it on, but dropped it when he saw how bloody the car was.

He say, "Let's put Silver back in the car, drive downtown to the hospital, and park there—in front of Emergency."

Rufus countered: "Naw, blow everything up! Torch the car and the corpse." But Fredericton was too near to try such a pyrotechnical scheme. Rue sneer, "Leave Silver here. If it snows, the snow will cover up our tracks and he'll disappear and the Mounties won't have a body and won't have a case."

George ask, "What if wolves or dogs dig him out, gnaw on him?"

Rue growled. "And what if the cops find him?"

George was sad: "Shouldn't've slugged im."

Rue: "Shut up! Who's got the brains here?"

George: "Haps you shouldn't've done the braining."

Rue shrug. "Whole lot of us is gonna feel pain, sooner later.... Squeeze him into the trunk. Leave his ass in Saint John."

"What?" George's breath was explosive fog. He was scared, but flush with cash. He stared into the guilty woods. In back, there was bogs, brush, and forgotten graves.

Rufus decided: "You's gonna drop the man's ass and car down Saint John to smear suspicion on niggers and crackers down there."

The brothers went and picked up Silver. A sigh parted the man's lips, and they dropped him and scrammed. But they looked at each other, felt silly, and turned and saw Silver laid out flat, stiff, akimbo, in the snow. So they went back, hefted him up again.

Dragging the dead weight back to the car, Rue joshed, "Joyge, ya go down to 47 Moore Street, buy a heap of liquor. But when you're drinking, walk back, one room to the other— some here, some there—eyein the gals and drinkin slow. Then you choose one, and don't feel bad: every bed in that house has seen three generations of whores."

George nodded okay; he already had his mind set on one of them ladies, Lovea, even as he was manhandling the bleeding, inconvenient Silver.

The brethren now jammed, bent, and crammed Silver into the trunk. They squished his pint-size body into an ant-size space. Silver's head looked squashed lying against the spare tire and wheel, and his legs doubled up with the feet on the outside left corner near the trunk lid—just like that. He was partially wrapped in a Canadian Tire car blanket.

Tryin to squeeze Silver nicely into this unorthodox sarcophagus, George kept slammin the lid on Silver's frozen and bloody right foot. Panicky, he just kept mashin the trunk lid on the man's foot, thus continuously mangling the appendage. Groans came from Silver, and that just made Georgie feel worse. Rue pushed the man's messed-up foot into the trunk and then slammed the lid. Then Rue tore up Silver's wallet pics of his cutie-pie wife and pretty kids and flung the man's crucifix deep into irreligious woods.

These two scions of the Dominion motored back to the gravel pit: a good hiding place for a car with a likely corpse in its trunk. Here Rue said Georgie'd feel better once he had a horde of harlots. George giggled.

Rue winked: "Doncha wanna see Lovea again? I knows ya went down to Saint John last month to see her cause you couldn't get pussy from big-belly Blondola. Now, with the stash ya got, you can taste Lovea. She's real tangy!"

Joyge ask, "How ya know that?"

Rue was sly. "Ya gotta work her sweet thing like a horse."

Rue and George only had to pass through a screening clump of bushes and a thick double stand of pines and spruce to get from the gravel pit to their shack, only about a hundred yards in all. When they come, bloody, into the house, they was expecting to find Plumsy Peters there. But Plumsy'd decamped, leaving infant Otho all alone in his crib. Nicely, Otho was snoozing nice and sound. The fire just needed heartening—to warm Otho, yes, and to burn up guilty things. Georgie freshened the fire. Then the boys got rags and two quart milk bottles filled with soapy water.

They went back out into the cold night and set to launderin the car upholstery. George washed one side of the car, Rufus the other.

George simpered, "Silver's blood's fuckin everywhere." They slaved like Cynthy had, dying, scouring a pimp's toilet. Look, Georgie and Rue were both on their hands and knees, panting, working hard to clean up the blood. Horror: the blood fuckin leakin through seats, spoutin through upholstery, as if two no-brainers had turned on a tap. They was spongin up blood (sloppily). They poured water into a milk bottle so they could do a lackadaisical job cleanin up blood by flashlight.

They trashed the bottles and rags in the snowed-on gravel. Back to the house they went. Water slithered from a tap, coiled at the drain, vanished. Four red hands divided the flow. Rue stripped off his overalls and stuffed em and the hammer into the stove. George incinerated his own clothes too. Rufus demanded the watch and wedding ring from Georgie.

He said nope: "Lemme sell em."

Rue snapped, "When Silver's car is found, the cops'll look for the watch and the ring and they'll be evidence." Both trophies got dropped in the stove.

George told his brother, "Now I've got money; you've got money. How about you going fifty-fifty with me on some food and wood?"

Rue say, "Gotta get my clothes out the cleaners." His smile was moonlit. "When money changes hands, it changes minds." He told Georgie to scoot to Saint John, drop the car, take the first bus back at dawn. But first, George should run him up by Minto so he could set up a gamblin alibi.

George said he'd do errands, then pick up Rue.

George motored to the Community Lunch, parked down the street, went in, settled a bill. He saw Plumsy there and told him to go tend Otho, that he'd get top dollar and lots to drink. Rum was not just Plumsy's vice; it was his consciousness. So Plumsy donned his moth-chewed coat and lumbered out. Then George drove to Gus's and Russ's and bought Coke and apple pie and sat and ate—to revisit and then satisfy his day-long hunger. After that, George hummed back to the gravel pit, parked, then scrambled up a small hillside of bushes and the stand of trees to go back in his house. He thought he should go back, unlock the trunk, and check to see if Silver had started breathing again. But he was scared of likely facts.

Back at the shack, George come in and see Rue sitting, real easy, with Plumsy. Both were drinking beer, talking about nothing. Then, coolly, like he wasn't worried about nothin, Rufus pulled out his nice bulky wad of bills, said, a tad drunkenly, "George, show Plumsy your money."

George shook his head no. "Ain't got no cash."

Rue glared at George. "Plumsy ain't no cop. I told him already about the score. Now, show him your half."

Plumsy looked at George eagerly, and his glance communicated pride: could Georgie really have socked a taxi driver and sacked his cash? Seeing that admiration in Plumsy's face and the tension in Rue's, George slowly hauled out the wallet, thumbed through it, displayed George VI's five-, ten-, and twenty-dollar faces.

Plumsy whistled low, appreciative. "My, Joygee, looks like you got more cash than Rufus."

George say, "Plumsy, if any questions come up, tell em Rufus was home all night lookin after Otho, while I was out gamblin."

Rue nixed that story. "No, that's my alibi! I'm goin up to Minto to stay all night."

Plumsy piped up again. "I'll watch the baby and all, but I need to bag more beer."

Rufus passed him four quarters. "That'll keep ya till we get back."

Plumsy ask, "How ya gettin to Minto?"

George blurted, "We got a brand-new Ford back in the pit."

Rue nodded: "We took the man's car, too." Rue sucked the last of the beer.

Plumsy yelled, "Hey! Isn't ya leavin the rest of the beer for me?"

Rue withdrew a fistful of silver from a pocket: "Don't sweat it. We'll see you fixed up for that."

IV

Now early, early morning of January 8, 1949, the boys felt compelled to trudge back to the gravel pit, open the car trunk, and diagnose Silver. They was hoping he'd sit up, teeheeing, asking what Sambo joke they were playing. Silver's eye glared up at em. The brothers closed the trunk, but George, fumbling, couldn't lock it. He couldn't get the key to turn.

So Rue stomped on the trunk lid with one foot, then turned the key in the lock: "Joygee, go to Saint John and throw the keys in the harbour."

Leaving Plumsy at the house with Otho, George and Rue wheeled to Minto. George wore Burgundy's dark taxi cap. It felt good. Rue tried it on, rakishly, like a jazz man. The moon minted four copper pennies in four eyes.

In Minto, Georgie stopped at Junior Clarke's place.

Rue knocked, yelled, "It's me, Junior."

Junior shouted, "Show your mug at the window." Rufus stood at the window; a curtain swished. Then Junior cracked open the door. A big fat fellow.

Rue ask, "Got a game on?"

Junior said, "Show your stake." Rue flashed his blazing bills.

Junior: "Okay. You cheat, I'll bust your ass!"

Rue say, "What?" Junior weren't amused.

Leaving Rue in Minto, George drove along the road back toward Fredericton. He saw a hitchhiker and stopped for him, a large-built fellow, this French chap whose English was shaky. He was a giant version of the little man in the trunk.

George ask, on impulse, "Know where I can get liquor and a gal?" The hitchhiker—Willy Comeau, ex-lumberjack—was scared of George. He feared he was a cop cause of that official-looking cap. George said, "I's a taxi driver! Ain't no cop! Ya know any Negro cop?" Both him and the French man roared at that gag.

Willy told George to go down a side road and up a hill and into a driveway and turn his headlights off and on twice. He begged Georgie for ten bucks, and Georgie used the moonlight to figure out what a ten-dollar bill looked like and gave it to Frenchy. Willy rapped on a door and parleyed in Acadian. This other man, who never turned on a light and never left the shadows, went away from the door, then came back with a box and a bag. Willy returned to the car with a quart of whisky and two quarts of beer, or two quarts of wine and one beer. This was all the liquor Willy had in his hands. Between 2:30 and 3:00 on Saturday morning.

Then Georgie motored back into Minto, on a whim, to check on Rue. Willy tagged along. Back to Junior's went Georgie, arriving to see Rue leaving.

Rue was glad: "Junior just put me out cause I quarrelled with his rules." He saw the hulking, quiet Willy and ask, "Who the fuck are you in my brother's car?"

Willy only knew rotten English: "I's knows where fuckin booze is, chief." Willy showed Rue his cache of liquor.

Rue got into the car, opened the quart of wine, and give the big man a drink and took one himself and asked George if he wanted one. George said no, then let Frenchy out on a little hill by a store which sits on the right hand side of this road. Then him and Rudy boomeranged to Barker's Point, passing again through Fred Town. The moonlight rained like bleach—the way it cut through shadows.

Back home, at 4 a.m., the boys sat in George's kitchen, listening to Plumsy snore and trying to decide where to put that sluggish form in the trunk of the car parked in the gravel pit. Rue said again, "Best bet is to take the car into Saint John and park it there."

CURIOUS pilgrimage: to go into Saint John, used to receiving barrels of potatoes, barrels of apples, barrels of molasses, and barrels of rum, with a corpse that wasn't in a barrel. To pick up Highway 102—the Lincoln Road—to Saint John, George swung north up the Richibucto Road, driving right by Jehial's where Silver'd perished only a few hours back, to Marysville, headed east through the village, passing two-storey red-brick houses (accommodating Marysville Cotton Mill workers), to ford the Nashwaak River via Bridge Street, then turned south to cross the Saint John River and pass through Fred Town—and cross into a mug's history.

He was sure to be recognized. Here he was a notorious "local colour" Negro, poor, in a literally bloody taxi-driver's cap, driving a deadly new and new-smelling stolen black Ford sedan, a corpse in the trunk, and yet careering boldly along well-policed streets like ritzy Waterloo Row. Eventually, he veered onto the Lincoln Road, that nasty two-lane icy highway flowing windingly along the river to Saint John. And he did so half-asleep, half-drunk, and thoroughly spooked.

George talked to himself, explaining to the dashboard and the still slightly bloody upholstery that this, ahem, *slaughter* of Silver was really a kind of sacrifice to cleanse his own sins. Somehow those hammer blows were the death knell of his past errors and failures. He glanced at the cool, smooth

Crown-land—Government of New Brunswick—snow. It almost seemed to whisper as it slicked past in the moonlight, "You're okay, Georgie. That body in your trunk is like vanilla ice cream, and ice cream is good. You're A-1, A-OK, with a new baby girl who is just like chocolate ice cream." Because Silver had suffered this accident (no hard feelings), George felt he could convert himself into a teetotaller, a hard worker, a faithful husband, and a respectable father. Blood might be flourishing in the trunk, but George still considered it a virtual velvet casket, much like the one in which his mother had been buried. Besides, to commit murder, you had to have intended to commit murder, and no one had lusted to see Silver die. That he did expire, well, that was just *Fate* acting up. After all, George now had the money to redeem Blondola and Desiah, his newborn. Apparently, Desiah's birth had mandated Silver's death. There was a balance here. George told himself that, having survived Silver, he should now take Blondola and his kids and go, maybe, to Cuba, start over in a warm place of rum and Christianity, where lots of Coloured people looked just like him, and he could thrive as a jovial, harmonica-playing fisherman. Certainly, it now seemed very agreeable to drive by Stanfield Jackson's place, pay off a two-buck debt from three months ago, and put this ill-gotten cash to healthy use.

None of this philosophizing complemented Georgie's screaming desire to see Lovea, to smell and taste her, to feel her wet and soft, to hear her sigh and moan. But tonight—or this morning—was an occasion for tests, for experiments. He could be forgiven for trying everything now. If murder could summon redemption, then adultery could invoke salvation. George now vroomed faster—first to pay off Jackson, then to pay Lovea.

George stopped in Lincoln to get gas but couldn't rouse the B.A. garage man from a death-like sleep. In Upper Gagetown, he drove to a B.P. man—Havelock Gerrard—he'd known before, wheeled into Gerrard's yard, blasted his horn five, six times, until Gerrard come thumpin down from his bedroom above the gas pumps, bawlin Georgie out, and gettin, in return, only "Sorry" and a mollifying tip. George bought four dollars' worth of gas and gave Gerrard—forty-five, white, grey, and tobacco-smelling—an extra buck. Gerrard then sank two quarts of oil into the car: a dry engine. Inside the service station, there was a string, one used to lynch bologna, hanging from the ceiling. George could see it through the window. Ominous paraphernalia. He bought a package of Player's cigarettes, two Daily Double cigars, and a chocolate bar. George told scowling Gerrard to make the bill out to Elroy's Taxi, so he could get his cash back. (He also hoped the bill would serve as an alibi, suggesting Silver had loaned him his car. Indeed, there'd been no complaint from Silver.) Gerrard spotted a dark stain in the snow where the car'd been.

South, south, south, and further south, George swerved toward Saint John. He'd fortified his brains with coffee doused with rum. Drowsy, he stopped at Oromocto, in the parking lot of Acadia Distillers, makers of amber Governor-General's rum, and began to doze, his windows rolled up, the engine running. He was wakened ten minutes later by the distillery guard rapping on his window. Groggy, Georgie cranked the window a peep. Cold air hammered his face. The guard glared whitely in moonlight. "I thought you was dead. Shouldn't snooze with the motor on. Poison builds up, makes you feel sleepy, and you sleep, but don't wake up." George thanked the guard for the warning and started back to the highway. He almost forgot about Silver drowsing peacefully in the trunk. It was peaceful.

Fields blurry with January snow. Night greasy with snow, slick.

Four miles below Gagetown, Georgie turned off the road, took the back road leading into the Hussar Farm, then took the road cutting through Elm Hill—that old black village where land titles were a spaghetti dinner. He stopped at Rocky Jackson's house, woke up his buddy by honking, roused a barkative hound too, and did so just so he could ask befuddled, angry Rocky where his son Stanfield was, cause Georgie owed him two bucks. The dog kept lunging at the end of its chain and barking a blue-black streak in the night that was blue molasses with morning. Rocky yelled at his mangy mutt to shut up, but he could strangle Georgie for botherin him at this god-danged hour. No, he didn't know where Stanfield was, but he guessed he was with a woman—just like hisself.

"I got no business with you, Joygee!" To pacify Rocky, George give him a buck for himself and two for Stanfield. He'd driven down from Fred Town with a flock of dollars after a "cash windfall, no, eruption," he couldn't give details about: Ask him no questions. No questions got asked.

There was snow bulked up round the pines. The dog barked again. George slid away in the comprehensive night, all its stars ablaze, and set his mind on Lovea, her asking him that last time, last month, "Is your heart on fire?"

Nearing Saint John, George saw the nickel-plated river melt mercurially into the town. He was traversing a Nouveau-Brunswick of white darkness and dark light, a matrix of blizzards and shadows.

Arriving in Saint John (lousy fiefdom of a lumber-baron clan who slew whole forests to satisfy familial greed) about 6:15 a.m., Georgie careened through a cliff-slippery, hilly city, dramatically shuddering, crazy, toward the Fundy. He saw churches mushroom from solid gravel; teeter-totter houses see-saw up and down steep, cascading hills. He felt sensations of vertigo and inversion because of the Leaning Tower architecture. It was an interesting place to be drunk—like walking up a Ferris wheel. The two-storey-high Victorian wood-frame houses seemed set to tumble into the Fundy'd Atlantic. Here was a damn damp port. In town, he passed that true heart-of-whiteness, with dead citizens at its core: the Old Loyalist Cemetery, that graveyard crowded with traitors to the Republic. His engine throbbed, *failure: failure, failure*. Then he skidded down the long slope of King Street, capped by Birks, the diamond merchants, to the bottom corner suggesting a new Piccadilly Circus: the semicircle of the Canada Permanent building, its grey-brown cement face gazing paternally at the wharves and docks and tea-laden ships.

George considered that if he dumped Silver in the Saint John harbour, right beside him, it would constitute a burial at sea, a noble naval honour he'd seen practised frequently in the Merchant Marine. But he were scared to touch that dead body. No, let Silver rest, gleaming, in his come-by-chance tomb.

Georgie drove to Station Street, passing both the Lord Chamberlain Hotel and the Hum Tom Laundry. He crossed a gully to pick up Moore Street, right beside Paradise Row, a stretch of three-storey, dilapidated houses, well-designed for bootleggers and prostitutes.

George made a beeline for number 47. Where else to be on such a nightfall morning, save in the company of a woman in a house where men are expected to shut up or sing? The four-storey structure sat across the tracks from steaming train engines and the steaming, frigid harbour water, always indigo, perse, or slate grey. Right below Fort Howe, the hilltop cannon post loved by the British Navy when it was guarding New Brunswick from the grasping Yanks. Taxis'd always be at 47 Moore, so George's—Silver's—didn't seem unusual. After he parked at the back, stood woozily, and trudged slowly toward the front of the house, George jumped back as two humongous rats, squealing, flying, incisors and claws sweeping at air, fell from the roof and thudded into the snow at his feet. (In Saint John, the rats were so big that, when leaping from roof to roof, a few would miss and strike pedestrians, cars, or just the ground.) Then he had to sidestep stringy cats who streaked from shadows to bat about and maul and chew the struggling, gut-splattered rats. He turned and saw a mutt sitting under the Ford's trunk, lapping at the suddenly brothy snow.

George went up to the front door, tired from stress, and rang the bell. Dutchy, mean-mugged, tar-eyed, and tattooed, auburn skin, peeped through a peek hole, seen it was Georgie, let him in. George asked Dutchy for a pail of water and two towels to clean the "throw-up in the car."

George washed the floor of the car, the back of the car, the doors of the car. He ignored the trunk area, but had to keep shooing away that persistent, growling dog. The towel soiled with blood he threw away.

He took the empty bucket and the clean towel back into the house to Dutchy. He asked for and got a room with a window hinging on the harbour. The last moonlight glimmered. That moon seemed too white: the smell of Silver's blood was still in George's nostrils and its colour was staining everything. The very air was ramshackle; the walls papery, so he could hear colossal trucks mucking by, shaking beds that were already jittery from don't-give-a-damn couplings. The toilet case was sweaty; the shower tiles mildewed. Just when Georgie began to feel he could relax, the wind came up against the building, heavier and heavier, like hammers.

A rap at his door, and suddenly there stood Lovea, a vixen with copper hair and sable skin, smelling of cinnamon. She wore a black dress—but was heart-stoppingly naked underneath. She rolled off her silk stockings and draped them sultrily over the lampshade. Her little purse held lipstick, compact, rouge, and a mickey of rum, all of which she used briefly before slipping easily into the bed. George studied her hungrily. For twenty dollars and a pair of nylons, Lovea opened to him like a narrow, twisted grin: Lovea—a love. As his lust trickled into her acidly, so did Silver's blood trickle slippery onto the snow beneath the trunk.

With morning, Georgie glimpsed a city of oil refinery fires streaking the filthy Saint John River a dirty orange. He felt dirty. Lovea rolled over funkily and he got a cigarette-and-rum breath into his nostrils that jolted him stiff. Despite the rooftop, outdoor noises of screeching, falling rats.

Later, Lovea brought Georgie a breakfast of corn flakes and scrambled eggs and sausages and toast with marmalade and hash browns and Red Rose coffee ("good coffee—as good *as* Red Rose tea"). He spooned up only a few cereal flakes, nibbled at the eggs, toast, and meat, but gulped down the hash and the coffee. Lovea ask George to drop her and her little Heinz 57 mutt, Martial, at the dog hospital.

First, though, Dutchy ask George to run him up the Main Street liquor store at 9:30 a.m. The trip was necessary because, of seven other men staying at 47 Moore, one was a boxer within inches of going to jail and one was a wino within seconds of going crazy. The guys'd asked Dutchy to spot em for First Breakfasts, and Dutchy declared it Georgie's Christian duty to help. On Georgie's last visit, he'd run up a tab Dutchy'd paid. Now, in return, Georgie bought the entrepreneur seven quarts of wine and Assyrian take-out.

Returning to 47 Moore Street, Dutchy was concerned to see a dog licking at a big red spot in the snow where Georgie's Ford had been. Two small boys were shooing the dog away so they could make snowballs using the freaky, pinkish snow.

Dutchy ask, "Oil leak, Georgie?"

George nodded. "Uh-huh."

Dutchy whooshed out with his liquor, and Lovea high-step from the house and sail into the car. She placed the leashed, panting, yelping Martial in the back seat. Lovea sat in the front seat beside George. But the dog went haywire, yipping, yapping, sniffing, whining, and scratching at the divider separating the trunk from the passenger compartment.

Lovea ask, "What you got back there, pig meat?"

Georgie teeheed: "Yeah."

At the vet's office, he got out and opened the door—like chivalrous Silver—for Lovea. After she descended from the car and retrieved Martial, Lovea kissed George. She smiled and began to sashay away, her boots pinking the snow, while Martial growled.

She yelled, "Better eat up that frozen shit in the trunk!" George removed Silver's taxi-driver cap from his head and gave it to Lovea: a gallant gesture. She noticed dark stains on it, but thought it could be a snazzy prop. She kissed George again and then led the yelping Martial into the vet's. George watched her progress, then turned, bareheaded in the snowing air, back to the hearse he had commandeered, snow crunching underfoot. *You murderer*, the snow squealed. *You thief*, crackled the ice. George saw a stream erupting—like Christ's damning blood—down a close hillside. Eleven-thirty a.m. now.

Heading back northeast to Fredericton, he viewed torn snow, dry wind, harsh sunlight—then none. A vomit of white drifting snow turned the sun into a pale smear along the Lincoln Road. Flakes of snow were calfing. Winter heaped wind at the windows. The highway blanked out frequently. The road was a curse, snapping, snarling. Gloom and near-zero visibility.

Shook up, sleepy, Georgie lost control of the powerful sedan at Oak Point, caromed off the road and smashed up the front fender by running into boulders. He'd been doin bout seventy miles an hour in all that fog of snow and the fog of a head-bashing alcohol mist and the fog of no sleep and the fog of a disgraced conscience. Awake sharply now, he tried to back the car out of the ditch it were in, but couldn't. The wheels writhed and howled and spat snow, but wouldn't reverse the car.

Passersby stopped, heart-stoppingly, to help. A middle-aged white man and his thin, youngish wife determined that their truck—a red something-ton Ford, could salvage George's car. They hooked a chain around the bumper and hauled the sedan slowly out of the ditch. Getting the black Ford car out of the white snow ditch was a long, freezing struggle for the red Ford truck. Georgie was nauseous with fear the trunk would flip open, giving him a lot to explain. The trunk latch creaked, squeaked, but didn't let go, and then the car was on nice, white terra firma again. George said his thank-yous to his Good Samaritans, who took the ten bucks he proffered, then he said his goodbyes. He jumped back in the hearse with what felt like three inches of icicles hanging from the rims of his eyes. He now felt his living difference from Silver.

My pulse is tinny; his blood was brassy.

It was on to Fredericton, the car engine noxious, snow copying a hurricane.

George remembered he'd promised Rue he'd leave the car and its corpse in Saint John. But now that he was steering his fate, he could relinquish neither the vehicle nor its silent passenger. Dead, Silver was as close to him as Rue.

About two miles this side of Oromocto, Georgie met a Mi'kmaq hitchhiker, young, tan, black silk-haired, husky, with blue jeans, a salt-and-pepper cap, a backpack, and, dangling therefrom, a typewriter. The lad, Noel Christmas, bore all this weight jauntily. George offered him a ride. Noel was also bound for Fred Town.

George had to ask, "Why tote a typewriter?"

Noel said, "I'm a poet—like E. Pauline Johnson and Bliss Carman. Know em?"

Georgie: "Nope."

Noel said, "I'm goin to Fredericton to visit Bliss Carman's grave."

Georgie let the poet out at the outskirts of Fredericton. He moved down a by-road spiking off from the Wilsey Road, near the Dominion Experimental Farm, and parked in brush on the side of the road going up toward a train track (to which he was oblivious). He got out of the car, in swirling snow, and hurled the ignition keys into a brook. Nigh 2:20 p.m. now. He locked all the car doors but one (an oversight). He strode quickly to the Wilsey Road, abandoning a shiny black car, all that gleaming promise of America and prosperity, amid bush, brush, remnants of the raw Canadian Shield and the scraping, scraggly terrors of the Ice Age. In fine, the car was visibly out of place where it was.

George'd spotted a snowy owl at Saint John, hovering above the river. Now he observed a gull near Fredericton.

George walked further down the road when a truck, operated by Moses Klein, coming from the city dump, pulled alongside, so that black-bearded, heavy-set Moses could ask George where he was goin.

George said, "Victoria Hospital."

Moses: "Are ya sick? Ya don't look sick."

George: "I'm going up to see the wife and my baby girl."

Moses said, "Hop in."

George dozed for blissful minutes. For one hundred miles plus, he'd worn a dead man's cap, and had cried and got drunk in mourning, from Fredericton to Saint John and back again.

VI

GEORGIE visited Blondola at about 3 p.m. He stayed with her and Desiah an hour. He left money to pay Dr. Pond, he caught the bus to Eatman Avenue. No one was home. Everyone—Rufus, Plumsy, Otho—was at Mrs. Roach's. George joined em. It was the first time he and Rue had glimpsed each other since early that day. Their eyes hardly saw each other. Guilt was one reason, wine the other. (Rue was so blue-mouthed blotted, he be all blue-blasted.) Then, under a debris field of clouds, Rue left to go shopping.

After talking with Mrs. Roach awhile, George walked to the corner store and bought twenty-five dollars' worth of groceries, plus baby oil, baby powder, different things. He got home just in time to see Rue unwrap his parcels. George then ask for something for the house.

Rue said, "I've spent every dime and dollar of Silver."

Cranky, George said, "If you ain't goin to put no cash towards the house or wood, you ain't goin to eat none."

Rue chuckled: "I's goin to eat at Mrs. Roach's then."

George say, "Go ahead—until I tell Roach bout you and his wife."

Rue said, "Yeah, and I'm gonna tell Blondola bout you and Lovea. I bet you saw her last night, eh?"

George was flustered. "I got the house full up with food, and it's goin to stay like that until Blondola comes out the hospital, and I will get some wood on Monday. I'm goin to try hard this winter to see if the house can be kept warm and that the wife and the children has clothes, wood, and food, and you ain't goin enjoy none of it."

Rue guffawed. "You know, Joygee, all that money's tainted: t'ain't mine an t'ain't yours."

Rue laughed more. He opened a box and took out a new fedora—black, with a feather—and put it on. He tried on his new black overcoat, a black scarf, black galoshes on his new black shoes, and posed like a gangster. He admired his new black pants and the silver-buckled black belt (his keepsake of Easter) that set them off so splendidly. He planned now to leave piss-ass Fredericton and go back to pianissimo Halifax. He'd scoop up India and go to Montreal and settle and never banter with bozo Georgie again.

The sun hung before them like a gigantic noose swinging the world. Rue uncorked a slim, glimmering bottle of burgundy—delicious grapes of wrath—got two tumblers and poured a dash for George, a splash for himself.

"George, you did leave the car in Saint John, didn't you? And you did leave Silver's body where it was, right?"

George nodded yes and drank the red wine.

Then, Rue sliced him off a chunk of brown bread.

ROPE

*Écoutez: il nous est indifférent que ce soit l'un ou
l'autre qui ait commis le crime . . . , si un homme est
un homme, un nègre est un nègre, et il nous suffit de
deux bras, deux jambes à casser, d'un cou à passer
dans le noeud coulant, et notre justice est heureuse.*

—JEAN GENET

I

ON MONDAY, January 10, at 2:14 p.m., a brakeman, Hub Howard, walking in front of a creeping freight, spied a spanking-new Ford sedan awkward in the bush, saw that one of its doors was open, saw that a dog had been in there and shitted. Suspicious, Howard radioed the RCMP.

The Mounties' sensitive eyes spied ghost traces of blood at once. They called a mechanic, who unhinged and removed the back seat so they could peer inside the locked trunk. A locksmith cracked the trunk and then they called the coroner. The coroner, Sylvanus Mitchum, with the help of police officers who knew the taxi driver, determined that the body in the trunk was that of Nacre Pearly Burgundy, and that he was dead due to a blow to the head that was probably inflicted by a blunt object. The police photographer came to map out and snap the body; Mitchum examined it. An ambulance blossomed redly in the afternoon like blood seeping through a sheet. Then a black hearse—from McAdam's Funeral Home ("First Choice for Last Respects")—parked beside the black taxi. Finally, a tow truck arrived to bear away the comatose car.

Citizenry, cops, and always rabid politicians went mad after that railway brakeman found Silver's dinged-up car and cops eyed Silver's dinged-in skull. Folks turned edgy, narrow, and volatile. People locked up everything and wanted to shoot any suspect face. Pandemonium pushed to panic. Fredericton's two hardware stores sold out of shotguns and shot and new-fangled locks. Lights burned all night, pleasing the kerosene and kilowatt merchants.

The police suspected a gang. Their maniacal manhunt triggered, as usual, raiding of the Negro quarter—"camp"—of Barker's Point. Mounties had to check every outhouse, every sty, and looked ready to kill. There was vandalism as they entered tubercular kitchens and crippled bedrooms; the threat of vigilantism where they found ingenious stills. Carrying Tommy guns, they itched to spray the shantytown with bullets. Quizzical cops handcuffed every black man or boy for the routine third degree, but no movie-style roughhousing. Fact was, none was necessary. Them Negroes, even surly, I-don't-like-white-folks-none ones, had to clear their lives of this bothersome homicide. So folks gossiped about Georgie drivin the dead man's taxi, but it was easy to mix up Coloured guys at night. Sides, they figured the killers were smarter than a clown like Georgie.

After two days of shakin down Barker's Point, siftin through squalor, as the sweating cops saw it, and even haulin in riff-raff, the dragnet was annoyingly empty. Soon, blood-sniffing tabloids in Fredericton and Saint John, cities that despised each other (pitting the bureaucrats in one against the workers in the other), would be caterwauling in harmony. A stink sharper than the sulphurous, bad-egg smell of pulp-and-paper mills would rise up stabbingly like the shittiest stench of Hades. If the Negroes were innocent, every white man was maybe guilty. The case might drag on, putting re-elections at risk.

Then dawned the minor but scalding sunlight of flash-bulbs. Silver got front-page, red-carpet treatment in his casket, and hundreds of exasperated and vengeful citizens congressed alongside. The funeral cortège was a moving flotilla of black taxis from across New Brunswick. Mourners

motored graciously through Fredericton to the packed cemetery. Folks worried sick about their own flesh.

Tabloids acted grief-stricken. They was contrite about what
happened, wished they'd cared more for public servants like
cabbies. They commented about life withering like snow,
about the way light tears itself to bits, struggling through pines,
about how anyone's blood is always like a newborn's, pungently fresh and precious, about how rock could spill and fall
toward no end. They wept for a crushed yellow flower in the
funeral parlour, the mashed body of a fly.

Georgie saw em headlines; he felt sick bout all em smarting
feelings. Nausea shook him from clenched jaw to quivering
bowels when he thought of Silver displaying the photos of
golden Donna and his pretty, priceless children. Georgie knew
he could get all the entertainment in the world just by watching
his own babies play. Then he'd vomit tears because, my God,
Silver was dead and his moolah all pissed away.

George knew no theology, even less about law, but he treas-
ured one redemptive fact: he hadn't tagged Silver; no, he'd just
tagged along with Rue, who had. Georgie believed his part in the
scrape was just layin the hammered man's body aside, then takin
some bloodstained bills. George prayed, prayed, prayed, when
he wasn't drunk, when he was breathing in the milky new-baby
smell of Desiah, or when he was cuddled beside Blondola,
spoon fashion, staying warm, his hands cupping, gently, her full
breasts, while January worsened outdoors and Rue puttered in
the kitchen, so, so innocently, never registering any tic or sigh
about his and George's *successful* execution of murder. While
Rufus sat in the lamp-lit kitchen, guzzling red wine and waving
his hand back and forth in time to some soundless music,
George wept silently, but fully. If only he'd gone muskratting in
April, fixin traps in logs and lettin em catch their feet and drown,
he could've got pocket money, nice money.

Feeling his hot moisture trickling onto her neck, Blondola, so fleshily good and rose-smelling, turned and asked, "Is ya cryin cause we's poor, or cause you's happy to be a papa again?"

George nodded.

II

DETECTIVES Michael Evans—forty, wiry, and severe—
and Ishmael Stark—thirtyish, dirty, and squat—
visited every garage, pool hall, tavern, welfare office,
and brothel in the district. Sallow, with dark brown hair
streaked grey, Evans was a natural partner for Stark, who was
pale, with hair as black as shoe polish. The pair were like village
poets, scrutinizing every aspect of their fellow and sister citizens' lives, recording details, eavesdropping, jotting down info.
They were convinced the killer—maybe plural—of Nacre
Pearly Burgundy was a culprit who'd needed money but no get-
away car. Why leave a Fredericton taxi in Fredericton? They figured the murderer was local, didn't own a car, but knew the
roads. The two detectives fixated on Barker's Point, where taxis
were always shunting. They sucked up rumours—from citizens
like Yamila James, Jehial States, and Zelda King—that ex-con
George and ex-con Rufus were seen in Silver's company, in his
car, and with remarkable, miracle cash that'd appeared as suddenly as a blizzard. So, they'd converse with chatterbox,
chicken-thievin, high-steppin, firewood-stealin George. That
Coloured fellow were not, they thought, smart enough to murder and obliterate the evidence, but he'd surely help pinpoint
Silver's last movements. They brought George downtown,
with no promises or threats, only a wish for him to help them

reduce their honest ignorance. They knew he'd been in the car that night. What else happened?

George took scared, but glued himself to his alibi, telling the Mounties he was gambling all night on January 7, 1949, but had gone to Jehial States, with Silver, lookin to invite him to see his wife and newborn girl. He'd had Silver drop him off at Barker's Point, maybe, must've been, bout 10 p.m.

"That's the last I seen of him."

Stark and Evans let Georgie go because they had no evidence, and Georgie had a newborn. The next day, January 12, George was asked back to the RCMP depot for a few more questions. All day he waited to be questioned. No one got around to it until that night. (The delay was deliberate—to give his conscience time to sober up and to make him feel too tired to lie.) The ceiling lights in the corridor bit like barbed wire into his eyes. The cop station bristled with filing cabinets—as if the files held the real firepower: an accusatory bullet for every man, woman, and child. George cheered up when Evans, wearing grey pants and a grey-pinstripe black vest, and Stark, in a black suit and tie, finally showed up, apologizing extravagantly, carrying big mugs of coffee, even one for him. Then they entered, all palsy-wellsy, all swell buddies, the interrogation room.

Evans and Stark were pleasant, respectful, in flattering ways that white men almost never demonstrated to Georgie. Evans pointed out, even before they settled down to chat, just chat, "Georgie, it's wrong to murder, yes; but history's full of wrongs." George felt vindicated, important. The slaying of Silver was sorry, yes, but not an earthquake.

Stark nodded. "Some things gotta be understood as accidents, not evils." What everyone agreed on was the need to preserve the beauty of family. Georgie could appreciate this, eh, bein a lovin father and a loyal husband. He could help Evans and Stark resolve this case and help Mrs. Burgundy and her children feel better about the "accident" that had down-sized their family.

His questioners were probing, gentle, and relentless, but not bullying. George never sweated his alibi. He said no incriminating word. His pursuers kept at him until five the next morning. They kept asking him questions gently, gently. Finally, George asked if he could see Blondola. The Mounties agreed, and an officer was dispatched to bring her from her bed, where she couldn't sleep anyway, down to the station.

Blondola and Georgie met alone in Evans's stacked-up-file-ridden and cigar-smoke-saturated and Scotch-smell office. When Blondola saw her husband, lookin child-like in Evans's swivel chair, and downcast, pain drilled her heart, for here she be, standin in the Fred Town Mountie keep, with her man in trouble, and two babes in her arms, sometimes looking at her and squalling, sometimes reaching for their father. She cried and she cried and she cried when George whisper her that story. She couldn't believe she'd let that obscene jailbird, Rue, into her house. No, no, no. Only one thing to do: confess Rue did it. Everyone in Fredericton knew George was a rascal, but no killer. But Rue? He was bloody trouble from the start.

Blondola say, "You and me, Jawgee, we was here for three years, doin well for ourselves, till yer brother come botherin us. Why should we suffer for what he did? Since all you did was take the dead man's money, we'll just pay it back, even if it takes you ten years. We'll pay it back, and Rue can go to Hell." Blondola sat beside Georgie, weeping. Her head rested on his shoulder like Silver's had rested on Rue's.

George took Otho in his arms and looked into that tiny face so much his own and he thought of Silver looking so glad to welcome he and Rue into his car. The tears shot from his eyes to join those of his wife, and he was seeing Desiah now, his brand-new baby girl, through a veil of blurring tears. As his hands fumbled over his babes and his wife, and hers stroked his face, he could hardly breathe, but managed to croak, "You go home now, Blondola. I'm gonna come home too. After I tell these mens what Rufus did, I'm gonna come home too." Blondola looked at him close. "You sure, Joygee? You sure?" He nodded and explained: "I took Silver's money, but I never even scratched Silver."

Blondola and the children left. Then Evans lunged back into his office.

George's *mens rea* was fully engaged now. He asked the coppers to bring a pen and paper to take down his statement: he couldn't print and weep simultaneously. Next, he told them everything—they pressed him to tell them everything—that incriminated Rufus, omitting only his own adultery. Lovea became a "friend" to whom he had kindly given twenty dollars and a pair of nylons.

George led the amiable Evans and Stark to his house and dredged up, while a frightened Blondola observed (and while Rue was out, sporting or drinking), the charred ring, hammer head, and watch from the stove ashes. The watch was still silvery and the ring was still gold and the hammer was still black amid the heaped-up ash. Back in the gravel pit, George helped the detectives retrieve the smashed milk bottle shards where he had so feverishly scoured away Silver's bleeding. They'd had snow kicked over them, but George pluck em up easily. He pointed out the site where he'd halved Silver's dough with Rue; he mentioned he gave the cabby cap to Lovea Borden in Saint John. Later, George directed the Mounties to Minto, where he showed them to Junior Clarke's place and to the house where he'd gotten liquor with Frenchy. At Oak Point, the cops combed the site where the car'd slid off the road. In Saint John, George had to beg an infuriated Dutchy and an anxious Lovea to answer intimidating questions from Evans and Stark. Back on the by-road near the Experimental Farm, George located the car keys in the brook. He fix a damning case against his brother, including the grisly detail about Rue picking up the dead Burgundy's black rosary and crucifix and hurling em into the woods.

George co-operated uncomplainingly with the Mounties. He confessed easily that Rufus James Hamilton murdered N. P. Burgundy. Still, the cops charged him with capital murder, despite all his charitable, earnest testimony and general good citizenship.

When the Mounties rolled Georgie's manual digits, all ten, in the fingerprint pad's black ink, he knew he was indelibly, incurably, black. The ink tingled like acid.

Then, too, the inescapable difficulty was that *he* and Rue had gone out for money and got a man killed. The saintly Silver—a veteran—'d been bludgeoned dead for the sake of $180 or so, his wallet depleted, his crucifix tossed wantonly in woods (where it ended up in a police dog's jaws). George was deeply micked up in the affair. He'd admitted he'd called the taxi, but why couldn't the police, the press, the court realize he'd never hit a man in his life? Didn't they know that when it came time for him to bash Silver, he couldn't do it?

"I had intentions to hit. But I couldn't—and didn't—slug Silver."

Was it his fault Rue was a bad man to leave on a road alone with a hammer in his hands? He wished he were home facing his "fambly", not in York County Gaol facing the gallows.

George had three motives for aiding the Crown: 1) he hadn't brained Burgundy; 2) Rufus were a vicious drifter; he—George—be a daddy, a hubby, and a property'd taxpayer; 3) the police kept him well fed while he was singing. He was finally eatin good regularly. He didn't like prison, but he liked jail food, much of it home-cooked by wives of cops and sheriffs, wives who felt sorry for young men who'd lacked good mothering. George had pies, muffins, cakes; all the pop in the world; orange juice, apple juice; milk, tea, coffee; sausage, turkey, mackerel, chicken, tuna, hamburger, beef; cookies— peanut butter and ginger snaps and chocolate fudge; fresh bread and beans with pork and lard; even pineapple rings. He'd'd no idea that some people ate so handsomely.

The RCMP dispatched a car to get Rue, and it came back with a good-looking known felon who wouldn't talk and didn't want to talk to George. But Rue was most angry with himself for not foreseeing that George'd fuck up everything by driving the car back to Fredericton and parking it where it'd be spotted easily.

III

AT THE RCMP DEPOT, Evans and Stark lorded it over a small room made tinier by just one table, three chairs, one searingly bright light, and many shadows. George was given coffee regularly, but was not allowed to smoke because Evans and Stark wanted him to sweat for each cigarette he'd be allotted later. They were dressed sharp as usual. Evans's suit was blue serge, and he had a grey tie and shoes. Stark was also natty, but in the usual black clothes, a skinny black tie, and a white shirt. George was outclassed: he had on hobnailed boots and looked like a lumberjack. The detectives hulked around him, scribbling, taking notes, sipping coffees, and casting larger-than-life shadows. They were composing a *res gestae*, a spontaneous statement, a script that, with Georgie's embroidered answers, would one day be pressed into death-sentence paper and then wrung into hangman's hemp. The pair untangled every riddle, every puzzle, of this cheerless violence that was now being woven into True Crime literature of the most official and fatal sort.

Evans and Stark had foolscap sheets with typed notations verifying George's screwy army service, his Montreal fracas, his drab tool theft in Fredericton. They could look at the sheets, look at George, and not look happy.

Evans said, finally, "Georgie, Georgie, Georgie, everything you done before last week was chickenshit compared to this homicide."

Panic blizzarded hotly inside George.

Georgie asked, pretty please, for a lawyer, but Stark swerved abruptly on his black patent leather heels, his grey suit flashing, and glared, Rufus-like. "You can't purify this murder by hiring a lawyer!"

Georgie sank back, choked out, "I didn't do it!"

Evans, cordial, calm, commented, "We've got the unburnt head of the hammer, the charred head about the size of a hummingbird (but much, much heavier—and far deadlier than that weightless creature), from the ashes in *your* stove."

Stark interjected, "Tell us about the hammer."

George shrugged, gulped his coffee, and explained (omitting his past legal troubles with O'Ree), "I used this hammer for banging iron, breaking cast iron and selling it to people I was working for. I flattened the hammerhead by banging it on harder iron. I did it, flattened that hammer, breaking iron when I was working for the Jew, Abe Klein, here in Fredericton. I flattened that hammer myself and pounded one side. I used to knock up old stoves."

Evans leaned over the table and winked. "Like you knocked up your ol lady, eh?" George laughed: he thought it was a joke.

But Stark retorted, "Or like you knocked Silver in the head."

George replied, "Not me. Rufus."

Evans returned, "One of you did slay Burgundy."

Stark sneered: "Oh yeah, one of ya's 'innocent'; the other one's bad. Sure, sure."

Evans continued, "Was that hammer the one you—or Rufus—used?"

George bowed his head. "I know which hammer is mine because I only have two hammers."

"And you helped Rue hammer a man for his money?" Evans sipped more coffee.

George blurted: "The money we took off Silver—it was Rue's, it was mainly silver."

Stark bluffed: "Silver's death was a big murder done by a big fool. You let Silver freeze—or bleed—to death, and then you stuck him like a carcass—a carcass!—into his own car trunk."

George winced at hearing the word *carcass*: he saw Asa pointing accusingly at him.

"You were a huge idiot, Jawge, to travel with a hammer in your overalls with the likes of Rue about."

"Maybe," George answered Stark, "but I don't know what my story is. It isn't over yet."

Evans scraped back his chair. It sounded like an avalanche of boulders. "Why'd ya do it, Joygee?"

"I—I didn't do nothin. It was all Rue, I'm tellin you. I had nightmares filled with blood, knives, and being chased—just ahead of the murder," George sobbed. "Also, Blondola was in the hospital, and our first baby was crying and crying and crying. So I needed money, so I helped Rufus."

Evans now asked, "Was it light or dark?"

Geo explained, "Well, it was pretty dark, real dark. I recollected. Quite dark then."

Evans pressed on: "How was the murder executed?"

George blubbered. "So we—Rudy and me—hemmed and hawed as to who was going to hit.

So Rufus said to me, 'You got the hammer, so you hit him.' But I took scared, shaking inside of me, and I dropped the hammer in the snow, and I said, 'I know Silver. I can't.'" It was hard for Georgie to get his breath.

He sobbed wheezingly, sighing, "Ahhhhhh," "Ooooooh," but Stark shouted at the shaken-up, shaking man: "A convenient story—quite suitable after smashing Burgundy with a hammer!"

George shook his head negativizingly. "I ain't sittin here to make a good story."

He elaborated: "All Rue said after he hit Silver was, 'I felt his hands and face and they were ice cold.' Me? I can't be blempt. I would spend my life selling cream from cows I'd milked, if it weren't for Rue and his schemes. I could've red-capped; I could've gone to the Boston States! I didn't want him to sock Silver. We got in a half dispute. We had a little dispute over it."

Stark walloped Georgie: "What numbskull helps a brother to hammer a cab driver in the head for money to get his wife and innocent baby out the hospital, but insists on driving all night, like a hellion, all over the risky, icy roads of this province, to buy stockings for a slut instead?"

George was exposed. "Nothing. I did nothing. She spoke and offered me a drink of wine." Even as he lied, he could see, suddenly, Lovea's lovely rump. But, hearing his adultery put so starkly *and* mockingly upped his despair. He'd have to let Rufus down, let Rufus hang. He blurted through his racking sobs, "Rue was the person who influenced me to do this so we might take on a white man and take his livelihood."

Stark growled: "Sure, sure, this murder doesn't come with your fingerprints, your mitts, all over it, eh?"

Evans rested a hand on George's slouching, shuddering shoulder. "Georgie, aren't you concerned you're hanging your brother out to dry?"

Stark guffawed: "Naw, just hanging him out to hang! You and Rue are as dumb as two chimps typing out Darwin's *Origin of Species*."

George bawled. "I was scared Rufus'd put that hammer in my head next."

Having helped to break Georgie, Stark became conciliatory. He removed the hanky from his own tailored pocket and handed it, with flawless, practised chivalry, to the slobbering George. "We was disgustin—I mean, discussin—this here conversation. Why don't we clear up a few other things?"

George blew into the hanky, quaffed coffee, drew a deep breath, looked around, red-eyed, sniffling: "Okay."

Evans asked, "Did anything touch Silver before he expired?"

George could only shrug. "The hammer touched him." Then Evans handed George, compliant and eager and grateful, a cigarette.

IV

THAT VERY Thursday morning, January 13th, Rufus was arrested. Evans and Stark recovered from his effects a pistol (*sans* ammo); chewing gum; Player's Navy Cut cigarettes; *Cane*, by Jean Toomer; a Classics Illustrated edition of *Titus Andronicus*; and sheet music, bloodstained. They also confiscated Rue's suitcase containing a black suit, three bottles of wine, and a quart of rum.

Rue shouted at the grey gabardine topcoated and grey fedora'd Mounties, "You guys are picking on me because someone killed some white bastard? All this shit because of one lousy dead white bastard! Shit! Shit! Shit!"

Plumsy Peters went into the cooler too. Just for good measure.

George, Rue, and Plumsy was all herded—separately—into the east entrance of the jail, a two-storey grey-stone structure with wood-planked, tin-clad ceilings painted either cream or indigo, and placed into one of the four separate second-floor cells, with 1840-era solid wood floors hammered down with homemade nails. Each cell had white-painted radiators, red-brick walls painted black, and black-painted, inch-thick iron-bar doors, and back windows, generously sized at three feet high and two feet wide, but bisected and segmented by a double row of iron bars painted cream. Here light could sluice in; no one could slide out.

Torture was wrought by the jail's location—adjacent to the

grounds where the weekly farmers' market was held. That good food roasting, frying, right under the jail windows enacted the curse of Tantalus. Although their prison fare was tasty, George, Rue, and Plumsy could glimpse and smell, but could not touch or taste, that fresh-barbecued outdoor food—chicken, steak, beef, sausages.

Inside the York County Gaol, everyone's face got branded with the shadows of the bars on their cells. At night, like flowers, three inmates lay dead-like and curled. Not much to do in the joint but think and squabble with guards and pray. Those jail doors clashed shut as noisy as shotgun blasts.

George saw himself as distinct from Rue, for he, the elder, was testifying against Rue. Disquietingly, though, he and his brother were always brought to court in a pair—and always handcuffed together. Padlocked and shackled, the boys listed to starboard, then listed to port, as they shuffled from the jail to the court. Sheriff I. B. Lion and the police were telling Georgie they considered him as guilty of first-degree murder as the man George was doin his best to see hanged alone. So, together, the Hamiltons got used to the weight of shackles and the cold, grisly wrist kiss of handcuffs. The two brothers staggered; they were so cluttered and clattered with chains. They had to walk chained in the street, degraded, flanked by two jail-an-nail-ems. Rue tried, as often as possible, to trip up Georgie as they lumbered along. He hated to see his brother so nonchalantly trying hard to get him hanged. Their fighting was as soft as shadow-boxing, but no less fierce. Rue tried to swing himself about to trip and bruise George, to make that fool understand their chains were all his fault.

George say, "Rue, it weren't my arm that struck out a life, but yours that made a ruin."

Plumsy yelled from his cell: "Joygee, must you jangle with your brother so?"

Rue laughed bitterly. "Joygee, you think em laws gonna cut you some rope, and they will: but just one you gonna hang from."

George said, "No, you just talking bout your damn self."

Plumsy yelled again, "Joygee, you just a cocksuckin, bootlickin Uncle Tom, actin all sissy for the cops."

Rue guffawed.

George was furious. "Listen up, Plumsy. I just hate the way the cops hate us."

Rufus snorted: "Don't hate their ways; hate them back."

Instead, George deviously secured religion. He was already a Crown witness; now he'd witness for Christ. So he signed the Articles of War, confessed his sins and love of Christ, and enrolled as a Salvation Army soldier, thus joining the same faith whose members had befriended him when he was locked up in London and Montreal. He figured he'd have more success in this army than he'd enjoyed in the Canadian one. Besides, the Sally Ann was —just like Christ—used to treating with thieves, prostitutes, gamblers, and drunkards.

The Hamiltons entered the York County Courthouse like a deuce of devils, with George's piety contrasting unhelpfully with Rue's disdain, and with George's religiosity disguising a Rufus-like rufous and ferrous disdain. But nothing could allay public outrage. Whites were feelin shaky now round their Coloured cleaners and cooks and maids: "Negroes could be annihilators—despite their giant smiles!" Whites didn't like the idea of grinning, killer niggers. So the boys became solid idols for popular fury.

Newspapers thudded like slabs of beef against the jailhouse floor. They warbled lustily of this murder drama. "Negro thugs with hammers"; "Coloured crooks with blonde tarts." Reporters called the brothers Scarface Titus and Pretty Boy Macbeth; they mixed "God Save the King" with a few bars of "Dixie."

Letter writers to opinion pages cried for blood, as did at least one poet:

"The brain exploded. The occipital busted ugly / —as if the hammer were of such a gross calibre of overkill, / it was a Hiroshima-style bomb: / Violence to devastate not only a big city, / but much of a country besides."—*The Fiddlehead* (Fredericton, N.B.).

The tabs used scowling photos of them condemned boys. The pics were silvery formaldehyde fixing the cons in brilliant infamy. But editors knew that no matter how bad those negatives were, Silver's autopsy photos were worse.

The two Hamiltons appeared as black as sin. No one could whitewash their atrocity into a mere mistake. Two scions of Three Mile Plains had to perish, *suspensus per collum*. They had to die at the speed of light, shadowed.

V

PLUMP, GRIMACING, his Conservative skin tweeded over, Mr. Justice Jeremiah Chaud, under his black robes, presided over York County's fake Grecian courtroom like a squat smokestack stabbing through a plaster Acropolis. He bossed his realm like a slightly less portly J. Edgar Hoover. Raised in Miramichi, his parley was as beautiful as italic script, but also as dark-edged as letters on a Gothic headstone. Sharp words aimed like knives. As an utterly English Acadian, with not one particle of French that he could pronounce properly, as a soul who was now sycophantically subordinate to the remnants of the original Anglo-Saxon empire, he felt it was his duty to ensure that the poor—and all those who were not purely white and English—stayed in their fetid stations: the Mi'kmak, the Acadians, the Negroes.... Under the twisting fan above his big head, useless in the May heat, he swept his perspiring face incessantly with his napkin.

For Chaud, as for anyone, the Hamiltons' alleged crime was senseless; it had left a young father dead on a deserted road. Silver had been struck like he was a domesticated beast, just for a zoot suit, and bejeezly-bad wine. Then followed that Kafkaesque spree with the body. But the killers' colour was not immaterial: it made a black crime even blacker. Chaud had to wonder, "Is a Negro's laugh pastoral—or pathological?" That the Hamiltons were Coloured didn't alter the clear facts that two men had slugged, robbed, and murdered an innocent husband and father, and then outraged his corpse, all in cold blood.

Chaud's understanding was that the Hamiltons had got some beer and got fired up with a deadly lust for money to splash on wine and women. The ugly results of an unhygienic paternity, they were a strain of tramps, laggards, dullards, retards, with violent, cotton-picking hands that, if permitted, would level the Parthenon to a sty.

Chaud also understood that the brothers, if found guilty, would both hang, even if George'd never hit Silver a single lick. Under the *Criminal Code of Canada* it didn't matter who'd, individually, killed: the law was remorseless here. It took the view that Silver wouldn't've come to harm later if the boys hadn't planned on robbery initially, regardless of whether they'd wanted violence. "Good intentions" didn't count. That George may not've meant Silver to die, that he may not've struck Silver, that he was remorseful about what Rufus did, all these facts—if true—meant nothing. Section 69 of the *Criminal Code* was fatally clear on the point.

Whether or not Silver died instantly or after he was first laid down in the snowy woods for any animal to sniff and gnaw on or whether it was after he was lugged and jammed into the trunk of his own taxi, it was still homicide. Once the brothers formed the common, illegal purpose to use a hammer as a weapon to effect robbery, they should have known that murder would issue: hit a man with a hammer and it's just blood everywhere.

Thirty-year-old Crown Prosecutor Alphaeus Boyd—bearded, bespectacled, sleek, silk-suited—viewed the two brothers as one deadly criminal: Rufus-George, with suspect clothes, dirty looks, shifty grammar. Boyd heard a scintilla of Africa, of bush, in the boys' talk; also a hint of red men's hatchets, from before Europe's guns and cannons thrust Christ and Shakespeare upon the savages. Considering the case in his law offices, he scrupled to philosophize in his heart: "Are the Negroes oppressed? Yes. But they are not trampled in the streets or brutalized in their houses. Did the Hamiltons impiously procure Silver's death? The charge is more than credible." It was his job to coax George's testimony into a death writ against Rufus—and against the star witness himself. He could not forget either that his looming appointment as the deputy attorney general of the Province of New Brunswick could be withdrawn if the jury was not persuaded by the evidence and his arguments to bring mortal convictions against the boys.

VI

GEORGE'S trial was really Rufus's trial, save that Rufus didn't testify. Fine: for Chaud, Boyd, and his own lawyer, Wilfred Dickey (always celebrated for his Liberal-red ties and anti-Tory wit), Georgie described all he and Rue'd done in luring Burgundy out to the Richibucto Road and beating in his head, or, rather, what Rue had done in slaying Burgundy and what Georgie had done in stealing cash and a car and burning a watch and a ring. A fessed-up Sally Ann Christian, Georgie felt shielded by the truth.

The trial began badly though, for George attempted a comic-book-inspired defence he'd even concealed from Dickey. At the first opportunity in the witness box, he looked over at Chaud, sweltering in the standing-room-only courtroom, and intoned, confidently, "Your Honour, sir, I object of answerin any questions on the ground they might be discriminatin on me." When the courtroom dissolved into a chorus of hooting, big-top-like laughs, George was mortified.

Chaud had to drive the gavel down and down upon his desk and cry, "Order! Order! Order!" George swivelled around, bewildered.

Chaud then asked him, kindly, "Does the witness seek the court's protection?"

George nodded vigorously. "I'm pleadin the Fifth Amendment, Your Honour." More laughter, more gavel bangs.

Chaud explained that this court of law was in His Majesty the King's Province of New Brunswick, not in rebellious America. Too, *his* own proper *Canadian* address was "My Lord," not "Your Honour."

Rufus's lawyer, thirty-four-year-old Carl Waley, so dashingly Rue-stylish in dress and Rue-cool in rhetoric, grilled George hardest. He had to prove this boy's testimony balderdash. "You do crime for a living, right? You steal food and firewood."

George shot back: "I was doing penny-andy—*penny-ante*—crimes because I have a wife and baby boy and a newborn baby girl, but I never stole anything in Fredericton until Rufus come home."

Chaud harrumphed. "Aren't you despicably using your wife and babies as alibis?"

"No, Your Hon— I mean, My Lord."

Waley charged on. "You put all the blame on Rufus. Why?"

"You see, my brother thinks ahead of time. He knows about doing wrong. I thought Rufus was tops until he started acting against me."

Waley thundered, "Acting against *you?* What? You're the one who's testifying for the Crown and trying to hang your own brother. Why?"

"It has to do with the truth." George paused, and then he said fatal words: "I did my share and Rue did his. I am as much to blame as my brother."

Chaud, Boyd, and Waley took note of this "admission."

Questioning George about the testimony of Zelda King, Yamila James, Jehial States, and others, Waley asked, "Is it so difficult for you to accept the word of your Coloured neighbours, even when it counts against you?"

George pondered. "Sometimes, and sometimes ain't. We are Coloured boys, you see. I don't trust anyone in Barker's Point of my own colour. I don't trust any of em."

Waley pushed George further: "The fact is, on the night of January 7th, weren't you ready to hit a man quite dangerously to rob him and run?"

"As I explained before, I wanted to get some money." George shifted in his seat.

Waley demanded, "Can money bandage up blood? Can it paper over a cracked skull?"

"But I never hurt a fly and never hit a man in my life."

"Which is worse, to swat a fly or hammer a man?"

"Fly ain't a man, a man ain't a fly, but both like to live."

"When you dropped the hammer, as you claim, why didn't you let it lay?"

"Well, sir, poor people don't throw away nothing. Just because the hammer was gone, doesn't mean I was going to let go of it."

"You wanted that hammer to bang it on people's heads."

Chaud intervened: "Did you use a hammer for the same purpose before?"

George said, "Not concerning human beings, Your Honour." Guffaws convulsed the court. George added, smiling, "My Lord."

Waley continued his attack. "Didn't you know all of the taxi drivers in Fredericton personally?"

George was precise. "I knew 99½ per cent of them personable."

"So, no matter who would've answered the call, you would've been ready to hit and rob them."

"Just because I knew every taxi driver in the city of Fredericton, or in the world, does not say I like them all."

Waley, strut-swaggering back and forth, recovered. "Did you mean if it was someone you didn't like, you would strike and plunder them?"

"No. Do you like everybody you know personally?"

"What is responsible for the fresh details in your story?"

George stared back. "The truth."

"You claim that you told your brother to pick up the hammer you so coincidentally dropped because you were afraid Silver would see it. Now, why should Silver have been bothered to see you, dressed like a carpenter, with a hammer in your care?"

George inhaled, then half-whistled-exhaled. "We're Coloured boys, and Silver's with us on a lonely road with nobody else around and he sees one of us with a hammer: Now, what would you think?"

Waley sparred: "Isn't that prejudiced, a prejudiced view?"

"Depends on your colour."

Waley scratched for blood. "Didn't you go to Saint John to try to escape?"

George replied, "If I'd been trying to escape, I would've kept on going."

"You went to Saint John with a murdered man in the trunk of the car."

George admitted: "There was something wrong with my head."

"I'll say," snapped Waley. "Why did you decide to stop at 47 Moore Street in Saint John?"

George felt shaky suddenly; his nerves were rassling and jangling with each other; his bowels were backin up into his stomach. He said, "I wanted to pay Clarkie—Dutchy—a bill I owed. Clarkie was a great pal."

"After taking it from the pocket of a dead man? After coming from a car where a dead man's body was in the trunk? Remember to speak honestly: a half-truth can't be testimony!"

"I had the money and I had the debt." George felt a little better: maybe Waley didn't know about Lovea.

"You ate and drank and played music. Didn't you have some indigestion?"

"I did not hit Silver. I did not kill Silver."

"You didn't have any trouble eating afterwards."

"I never killed him. Why should I have indigestion?"

"It's cold-blooded behaviour for a killer."

"Rudy hit that man, not me. Why should I quit eating and drinking?"

"Why didn't you immediately pay the doctor's bill for delivering your infant daughter instead of driving to Saint John to shower a murdered man's money on a whore?"

Blondola's brown face flushed, then tears rushed her eyes, and she rose instantly and fled the court.

Watching his wife retreat, humiliated, George shouted at Waley, "Why do you need to disgrace me? I am disgraced enough."

Rue looked at his crying, voice-cracking brother and smiled, coldly, from the prisoner's box. Much tut-tutting in the courtroom.

"Didn't you spend the night with a whore? Didn't you go drinking and sleeping with another woman in Saint John, while your wife lay here confined in the hospital?"

George shouted, "Because of the nervousness of my nerves."

"You wasted considerable money in Saint John."

Georgie just shrugged, but he wept silently as he pictured Blondola fleeing the murmuring court.

Chaud said coolly, "The prisoner in the witness box will reply."

"I give her twenty dollars. There's no law against it. I'd have given all of Silver's cash away to get rid of it."

Waley shot back: "You drove coldly down to Saint John to dash the car and corpse. Instead, you took drinks and a dame at 47 Moore Street."

Chaud weighed in: "And you only paid the doctor's bill."

George nodded. "I bought baby powder, baby oil, flour, sugar, bread, butter, that sort of thing."

Chaud shook his head. "And you treated the whole Negro camp to booze with a murdered man's money."

Next, Georgie was asked to demonstrate on a papier-mâché dummy precisely how Rue had struck Silver. The plaster head busted, disintegrated. It looked like Silver hadn't just been murdered, but obliterated.

Summing up the case against Georgie, Chaud told the jury, "To me, the crux of the matter is, George practically hands over the hammer to Rue, thus guaranteeing Burgundy's bludgeoning. Clearly, the brothers were allies."

Plumsy Peters's testimony pounded more nails into two metaphorical coffins. He said he seen big spending by Rue on the murder weekend. Yep, Rue'd "got an overcoat out of the Boston Tailors, a new felt hat, a black jacket from Cash and Carry Cleaners on Queen Street, a case of wine (twelve quart bottles), blackberry brandy, and sheets of piano music. I figured he got cash from Georgie. So I asked Georgie, and he said Rue'd hit Silver an awful blow. I asked Rudy about it, he said, 'I'll twist Georgie's neck like a coat hanger.' I could tell the boys'd quarrelled badly."

Alphaeus Boyd asked, "Are you positive you were, at this time, sober?"

Plumsy joked: "I ain't positive cause I was drinkin."

Boyd offered a slurring aside. "So, you're a simon-pure Negro?"

Plumsy just shrugged. "You ain't proved opposite."

Waley told Plumsy, "You were thieving firewood. You don't like to work, do you?"

"I bet I worked more in my life than you have!"

Waley asked, "What were you doing the night Silver was murdered?"

"I was out stealing wood that night. I doesn't take a gang. I goes solo."

"You didn't change your clothes. You always wear dress pants when you go out thieving wood?"

Plumsy laughed: "Wouldn't you? It gives a ready alibi."

Rufus testified in his own defence at his separate trial, but his speech delivered merely cryptic satire.

Boyd asked, "Why are you here, Rufus?"

Rue explained: "Because my mama and papa made me—just like you."

Boyd tried again. "Does George wear glasses reading?"

Rue grinned. "I never seen him reading."

Rufus' replies so irritated Chaud that he asked Boyd, "How long will you proceed, Prosecutor, with this pilgrimage of the defendant? What has it to do with murder? I'm anticipating the finale of his music and tippling and tomcatting and smoking and so on."

Rufus sloughed off the proceedings.

Boyd noticed: "You speak almost perfect English, don't you?"

Rue smiled tightly. "I do."

Boyd retorted: "Are you allergic to the truth?"

"Ain't nostalgic for nothin, sir."

Boyd focused on picayune points. "You didn't mention you were a pianist at the preliminary hearing."

"The question wasn't asked."

"But you've mentioned it today."

"Because you asked me today."

Boyd queried Rue about Georgie's drinking habits.

"It's a habit of his. When he takes a drink, he believes in taking a good one. He goes straight for the hard liquor and will not pause for God—or man."

"How do you know?"

"Maybe I am wrong and maybe I am right. But it's a sobering thought to see him intoxicated."

Boyd then probed Rue's interest in India States. "Is she a white woman?"

"She is not Caucasian."

"Why haven't you mentioned her before now?"

"I've done everything I can to keep Miss States out of this turbulent situation. She is a respectable woman. We wanted to marry here at the Lord Beaverbrook Hotel, in a two-piano ceremony. She was going to wear a ritzy, white lace Victorian gown, while I put on jazz."

Boyd approached Rue with an exhibit, asked, "Do you recognize these buttons? They are from Silver's coat."

"These buttons could be off anything."

Chaud interjected, "I am comfortable letting the jury decide."

Boyd demanded, "Why did you use a dead man's money to buy clothing?"

Rue said levelly, "I didn't know the money belonged to Burgundy. The only face on it was the King's." The courtroom snickered. "As a Coloured man, I always strive to make a good impression."

Boyd asked, sneeringly, "Are you as delicate as a baby, Rufus?"

"My hands are priceless."

At the trial's end, George told the court, "The words in my mouth are too sad to speak.... When the court finishes, I will show that it was an accident. What happened. I study the Bible. It's horrible to look at the ground and just see dirt."

Rue pictured Chaud and Boyd as squid-like, inky, jetting Atlantic cold and darkness. When Chaud asked him to speak before the jury weighed his guilt, Rue said, with distinct gusto, "Nope."

Chaud had the last word: "George and Rufus Hamilton apparently hadn't worked for some time, but nevertheless had apparel and lots of feasting and alcohol—immediately after the crime. Silver is deceased due to the hammering of his skull. These two lusty Negroes *cannibalized* poor Burgundy. The verb is not too strong. One followed the other like a dog.

"Gentlemen of the jury, we have now reached the last scene of the last act of the tragic drama which was unfurled before you during the last four days; and this last scene is the rendering of the verdict—the true statement—by the jury, whose august solemnity will give the appropriate weight to the truth."

George glanced at the jury nervously. Their faces were all scrunched up. In the prisoner's box, Rue sucked his teeth and eyed the grimly praying, cockamamie, foolhardy George.

VII

AFTER THE JURORS reported, Chaud prepared to pass sentence. He began gently, professional. "George Hamilton, have you anything to say why sentence should not be passed upon you according to law?"

"I am a converted and convicted Christian, sir."

"Rufus Hamilton, do you have anything to say?"

"Nothing, sir."

Chaud glared at the obstinate man. "Nothing?"

Rufus stared back. "Nope."

Chaud harrumphed and launched into his lethal sermon. "It is a satisfaction to know that the poorest man, whether he belongs to the Caucasian race or not, may expect an able defence, which you lads have received. You are not of our race. That is no fault of yours. Whether it be a misfortune, it may be a matter of opinion. Your people were not brought here at your own instance or desire. Your ancestors were forced from their native homes, brought here to this land, no doubt against their own will. You are not to blame; you may be pitied for your colour and your race, but you and we have this satisfaction, that the Coloured man, the Negro, has precisely the same rights in a British, a Canadian, court to Justice that the purest white man could have.

"Indeed, I am glad that my people, the Canadian people, have that self-restraint which is characteristic, I think, of our people, and they refrained from doing violence to you, leaving you in the hands of the law in the regular administration of the law. That is a great object lesson to other people, south of the border, by whom you people are less humanely treated. You differ from most of us in blood, in race, but no man can say that you have not had a fair trial.

"Now, I must carry out my duty as prescribed by that impartial law that smiles upon all British subjects. After your fair trials, your juries have spoke, and so must I.

"Your deed constitutes a sickening chapter in New Brunswick history. You were without money, which is unfortunate; you were without mercy, which is unforgiveable.

"George, you say you have been converted. Good. Now, you will meet your Maker. I hereby sentence you, George Hamilton, and you, Rufus Hamilton, to be hanged on July 27, 1949, between midnight and noon, by the neck, until dead. May God have mercy on your souls."

George wept and shouted, "Praise Jesus!"

Chaud retorted, "Your brother may have trapped you into this final downfall, but you were already imbrued in *crime*. You carried the hammer—the very instrument of this homicide—so you could help your brother rob and murder an innocent man. And it was you who took the slain man's money, divided it callously, and then helped to wash away and burn up evidence. If Rufus is the physical killer, you, George Hamilton, are guilty of making murder possible."

George fell to his knees. Rufus smirked.

Pandemonium rocked the court. Creaky old men leapt to their feet and cheered; one excited young blonde woman yelled, "We'll kill them in their very souls." Savage applause, whoops, cheers, with Chaud slamming his gavel ineffectively down and down.

Detective Stark, standing behind the weeping, crestfallen George and the nonchalant Rufus, leaned over and whispered,

"The gallows'll gut your necks, boys. You'll twitch, jig, piss, shit, sigh, and wheeze, and that's it."

Rue turned to Stark and said, smiling, "I'm ready to die. Are you?"

VIII

The Casket—Fredericton, N.B.
Friday, May 20, 1949, 4 p.m. edition

George Hamilton and Rufus Hamilton, Brothers, Were Given Death Penalty for Killing Taxi-Driver Nacre Burgundy of This City—George Made Statement

FREDERICTON—First to be tried for the diabolically calculated and most brutally executed murder in the history of this provincial capital, the dapper Rufus Hamilton was found guilty following a four-day trial, as was George, despite the fact the comical, local colored man took the stand for the Crown and blamed his younger brother for striking the death-blow, at the close of a three-day hearing.

Evidence brought out by newly named Deputy Attorney General and trial Crown Prosecutor Alphaeus Boyd disclosed that after slugging Burgundy with an iron hammer and robbing him at the foot of Poplar Hill, the negroes left the taxi-operator's body under a tree for some time before stuffing it into the trunk of the car and throwing the keys away. Later, after dropping his brother off in Barker's Point, George Hamilton drove to Saint John and back with Burgundy's body in the trunk, before ditching it off the Wilsey Road, not far from the Saint John River.

When asked if he thought his brother George was "trying to pin this murder on you," Rufus replied, with chilly gravity, "Under the circumstances, one could arrive at that opinion."

When asked if he was "trying to pin Burgundy's death on George," Rufus declared, "I'm definitely not."

Before sentencing, George Hamilton said, "I want the citizens of Fredericton to know that I have nobody to blame but George Hamilton himself for letting my brother Rufus come home and lead me into this. I have been converted and have been reading the Bible in the Gaol." His Lordship replied, "You engineered the scheme that resulted in Burgundy's death. Counsel has done all he could be expected to do on your behalf. You state you have converted; now, make your peace with your Maker."

When asked by His Lordship to offer a statement of his own, Rufus Hamilton replied, in a low but clear voice, "I have nothing to say."

Unable to obtain a seat in the courtroom, a feisty, local colored lady, Mrs. Mossy Roach, not only demonstrated her resourcefulness but brought a smile from men in the corridors when she left the building and returned about 15 minutes later with a chair of her own, which she planted firmly at the main entrance to the court and remained there throughout the morning.

In the accompanying photo, Rufus is obscured, his face—a ghost—utterly shrouded in black, save for a slight pale profile rising out of the ink. He appears in a vertical rectangle, cropped to suggest the frame of a coffin. In contrast, George appears affable, smiling, with a handkerchief peeping from his coat pocket. He has long arms and hands. His rectangular photo is also cropped to suggest a stand-up coffin.

IX

MAY 29, 1949. Georgie put pencil to foolscap and wrote longingly to the Governor General of Canada, Harold Rupert Leofric George Alexander, or Viscount Alexander of Tunis, or His Excellency, the Administrator of the Government of Canada, to beg for his life. His tone: a supplicant's saccharine mixed with a suicide's cyanide. "So Sir that why I am humbling my self to You and Bagging you for my wife sake and two children Sake and for the good that in me and the new life I found in our Lord and in the name of Jesus Christ I Bag you sir to Spear my life."

Unfortunately for George, Mr. Harold Alexander—once the British army's youngest major-general, one who helped defeat Erwin Rommel's Afrika Corps, and the cool engineer of two celebrated troop evacuations during the Anti-Fascist War—loved fishing in Manitoba and hunting in Quebec: a kind of Group of Seven outdoorsman, he was not the type to expend mercy on a snivelling killer.

In his letter, George swore to be "a good Canadain and preach the Word of God to others" because he was "a christian at heart" who'd given up "smoking and Reading filthy books." He was "praying night and day so that you will see the truth in my Latter to you Sir" because "I am no murder or had no <u>intention</u> in my heart for it my brother kill <u>silver</u> with out me noing about it, and I no if I had not drop the hammer my Brother would of hit him with the beer bottal he had but I had comited a sin a mixed up in a crime witch in breaking the English Laws of Canada and I sin against God."

Georgie was "constantly Reading my Bible…the book that brought peace and joy to my Sole." George asked Alexander of Tunis to "pordon my wrighting Pleas Sir and my Spelling" and to let him have a second "Chanch." He "amitted" that he did call the taxi, though he'd "never hit a man in my LIfe so when it came time to that I was *supposed* to hit him, I could not do it." He clarified that "I am not guilty of hitting any Body in my LIfe, and I never planed with my Brother to kill any body . . ." but "I did planed Sir to go out and get some money and hit a man that is the truth."

Georgie pleaded for his dream future and that of his children: "I am a good man at Heart I never wanted to hurt any body in my Life, Sir my two children and my wife I am setting here thinking what my children is got to face if get Hang people will tell them your father was a murder and was hang I am not no murder sir but I was found guilty, but I ask you sir please think about what will happen to my children, this is something I did not want to happen to them, I wanted to give them thing I never had and bring them up wright and give them a Schooling, and learnt them wright from wrong and build them a house, for my wife and children, but my Brother Rudy lead me into a trap and spoil all that." George pleaded with His Excellency, "the Wright Honarble Govner General," to save his life. He signed off as "your Truely Slave George Albert Hamilton I thank you sir with all my Heart and Soul."

George's letter overlooked, however, what Viscount Alexander—who'd just toured the University of New Brunswick and snagged a doctorate—could not: the body of Nacre Pearly Burgundy had spawned a host of bitter citizens clamouring for two black boys to swing from a beige fake tree. (Indeedy, Fredericton was anxious to see "shiftless, murderous niggers" hanged—in tune with the racket of hammers hitting nails, the crescendo of piano keys—hammers—striking chords and the machine-gun of typewriter hammers striking paper.) The greatest ex-general (since the Duke of Wellington) of His Majesty's forces would bow to New Brunswick public opinion, which could be polled, while reserving respect for God's opinion, which no one could divine.

X

GEORGE began now to keep a journal, erratic Grade Three spelling and all, for his Sally Ann brethren. Still, after a couple of months of steady Bible reading and letter writing, his style had improved. Too, George adored the supreme, democratic equality of majuscule letters. There was an implicit salvation in lending Bible verses and personal talk this *gravita*s.

"I DIE AT MIDNIGHT ON JULY THE 27, OF 1949 ON WEDNESDAY MORNING EARLY. WHEN YOU READ THIS I MOST LIKELY WILL BE DEAD, BUT DON'T BE ALARMED AT HEARING FROM A DEAD MAN...

"I DON'T MIND TALKING ABOUT DYING ... I'M REALLY HAPPY.

"READ YOUR BIBLE AND YOU WILL GET ALONG IN THIS WORLD AND IN THE NEXT WORLD TOO. Eat every Honeyed page of the Good Book...

"YOU SEE I WOKE UP ONE NIGHT SWEATING ALTHOUGH THE CELL WAS COOL I NEW SOME BODY WAS IN MY CELL AND THAT WAS THE

SPIRIT OF GOD HE SPOKE TO ME AND SAID TO
ME WHY DON'T YOU BELIVED IN ME IS IT
BECAUSE YOU CAN'T SEE ME You BELIEVE
THERE IS A KING george vi AND YOU HAVE NOT
SEEN HIM, SO NOW WHY DONT YOU BELEIVE IN
ME, WELL I COME TO YOU TO NIGHT IN YOUR
DREAMS AND HE DID AND HE WAR A LONG
WHIT ROBE A THORNY CROWN AND WAS BLEED-
ING IN HIS BROWN HANDS, SIDE, AND GOLDN
FEET AND THEN I KNEW THAT GOD WAS REAL
AND MERCYFUL TO SINNERS, NO BODY HAD
SEEN ME CLIMB FROM MY BED AND FALL ON MY
KNEES AND CRY LIKE A BABY TO GOD, I DONT
REMEMBER JUST WHAT I TOLD GOD THAT
NIGHT ON MY KNEES BUT I ASKED HIM TO BE
MERCIFUL TO ME AN EVIL SINNER, HE SAVED ME
THAT NIGHT I KNOW I'VE BELIEVED ON HIS SON
JESUS CHRIST EVER SINCE THERE WAS A SMELL
LIKE CINNAMON AFTER WORDS...

"NOW AS I SET HERE IN THE COUNTY YORK JAIL,
I AM GOING TO TELL YOU ABOUT HOW CLEAN
MR LION THE SHERIFF KEEPS IT, HE ALL SO RUNS
THE JAIL, AND LET ME TELL YOU ABOUT THE
GOOD FOOD HERE YOU GET STEWS AND BEANS
AND SOUPS AND JAM AND CHEESE AND MILK
TEA MEATS, AND I DONT CARE IF YOU GO ALL
OVER CANADA THIS IS THE BEST JAIL I HAVE
BEEN IN FOR CLEANESS, MR LION THE SHERIFF
IS THE GREATEST MAN IN THIS WORLD TO LOOK
AFTER A PRISONER, AND HE LET ME A RADIO IN
MY CELL AND A CLOCK, AND ANY THING THAT
MY WIFE (BLONDOLA) BROUGHT ME IN..."

XI

ON MAY 30, 1949, the very same day Chaud wrote the Secretary of State advising the judicial murder of the Nova Scotians, Rufus James Hamilton, just twenty-two years old, and "sorry to say" that he had two convictions, dashed off his own sally to the "Guvnor General of Canada." For his bit, Rue was "sorry to say this but I must: I have served 2 years in Dorchester penitentiary for a crime I was not at all to blame for.... I returned to this city only to marry a girl I realized I loved." He applauded his "able attorney," Carl Waley, for his careful "inventory of the events so that people would be convinced I, Rufus Hamilton, am innocent. I, the accused, did not take the life from a human being. I am sorry to say that I haven't a clue who killed Burgundy." Rufus was "a Young Man who had planned to get married on the 15 day of June 1949 and live a happy life because I was very much in love with the wonderful girl I was going to marry."

Rue could not fake "humbling," so he was brazen: "My Honor, the people of this City do not believe that I took a man's life—all for a couple hundred dollars." Such allegations were "lying evidence." Suspicion ought to be directed on Plumsy Peters, "a plain liar" who'd claimed to be "a Friend of Mine," but what a friend! "My Life Depends on You, Sir: On Rejecting False Evidence Presented Against Me in the Court."

XII

ABSALOM Tombs, a man who tore apart houses for a living, was the carpenter appointed by Sheriff Lion to construct the spindly wooden instrument to kill George and Rufus. The splendid gallows grew spidery, then elephantine, inside the prison's barn. Tombs had to saw and hammer together a contraption—a dextrous machine—that would snap two necks elegantly. His work did not end until—like a tailor—he measured both Rue and Georgie for their separate box-suits of plywood (dead men's overcoats), which he also had to knock out. This latter task was simpler and cheaper than the first: that had been architecture; the second duty was just a hatchet job.

Mr. Arthur Ellis, the Dominion Executioner, based in Montreal, now had to mastermind a double hanging. Always snazzy, he sported a jaunty bowler hat and a Scottish wool suit in winter and a Brazilian linen suit in summer, and aptly white gloves. When on the job, Ellis secreted a pistol in the waistband of his pants. He liked big cigars, lemonade, beer (never when working), and Dixieland jazz. He'd retire in a few years—after officiating at more than six hundred "danglings" in Canada, the United States, Great Britain, the West Indies, and Palestine—to the Okanagan Valley, in pastoral British Columbia, where he'd become a first-rate cultivator of peaches.

XIII

WANING July light infiltrated maple leaves and one-foot-thick back-wall cement to sift through barred windows and spill shadowy across two telegrams confirming that Mr. George Albert Hamilton and Mr. Rufus James Hamilton must hang early the morrow. His Excellency must let Dominion Law take its local, provincial course. Sorry. Quite.

The quality of that light was yellowish and hellish, but it was still light, and the brothers prayed it would last forever. But the afternoon's shadows reminded George and Rue of the spectres of the previously hanged. These wraiths seemed to dangle from the ceiling pipes and to smile back from the reflections of themselves displayed in the water in their toilets. They were shades of spooks looking at spooks of shades, amid siftings of light like the dust of blossoms.

Outside, the green grass glittered; ants moved quickly. They seemed huge and fast to Rue's eyes. He sat and scribbled his one and only poem, "Three Killers":

> *Three white men*
> *are coming to kill us.*
> *Their ties are upside-down nooses.*
> *Their faces hammer breath.*

Three Kings of Killers—
Absalom, Chaud, Ellis—
will coolly kill us.

We'll don a new black skin of flies.

(The gallows swallows you whole:
You wallow inside its hole.)

—*Rufus "Jesse" James Hamilton*

George was most content. He had his Xn resignation. He heard the lush, velvety voices of singers amid wheatfields and tasted the sweet, pure wellsprings of the Bible. He figured his soul was polished pristine. He dreamt a Heaven with feasts of Syrian apples and Israelite quinces, almond-flavoured peaches, jasmine of Aleppo, cucumbers, lemons, sultana citrons, apricots and cottage cheese, pumpkins and pomegranates, white roses and rose-flavoured pastries, rum-laced pound cakes, iced nougats, lime sherbet, tarts, oil of lavender, caviar, grappa, champagne, red wine, eggs, roast turkey, venison stew, rhubarb pie, sausage, clams, lobster, any soup he could imagine, Montreal smoked meat.... Death would thin out his body, but Heaven'd fill his belly eternally.

Unlike George, Rue was coming to his death with an empty heart and empty hands. He wanted to believe he was beset by a demon that'd created a preposterous lie about him. (He thought heresy might displace hearsay.) Once the almost–Duke Ellington of Three Mile Plains, Rue'd now perform a *danse macabre*. He'd practise the art of being dead, his head splashed against hard air. After hanging, personally he wished he'd just be cut down, not dissected, disgraced, but flung into the closest marsh.

Rue thought—wildly—of India. He almost believed—had to believe in this sole redemption—that he had only desperately wanted to love, like breathing in fiery, milk-sweet air. If he could have interrupted India in her maternity, if he could have brought her bodily—beautifully—before him in her gold flesh and golden ways, Rue'd've said that she could take light and give it new meaning and he'd've admitted to her that when she sang out those fatal words, *I love you*, her heart was broken and his was not whole.

The alarm-clock hammer berated him, announcing, "You will die, you will die. Tomorrow, July 27th, in the a.m., you will die. You will never see the p.m. of that day." It wasn't hardly worth Rue's while to wake up.

Father Bataille from St. Dunstan's Catholic Church, across the street from the York County Gaol, was porcine, greasy, with a turpentine smell and a vile face. His sermons was worse than his hygiene. Still, the flushed, spectacled, peach-faced priest tried to preach to Rufus. He spoke of the ruins of love in some broken words, of the terror in the soul that no sermon expiates. Only Christ Jesus could help now.

"Don't you know the need of the Church in days like these?"

Rufus replied, "Don't you know the need of a man for a woman?"

Bataille persevered. "Be *yes* in the eyes of God and *no* in the eyes of Man, not *yes* in the eyes of Man and *no* in the eyes of God."

" Father, stand me on the gallows. I prefer it to lying in shit."

Rufus remembered those good times when he'd been alone, with half a piano, but a whole heart, creating, creating. Oh what he wouldn't give for a taste of rum! Bataille asked Rue if he had any remorse for the murder. Rue teared up, rueful: "I stole two hundred dollars once. I tell you it required nerve. I used to complain about cockroaches and mice. Georgie and me lived in a shack, dirty, cold. Our flowerbeds were graves."

Bataille shrugged, crossed himself, then exited. He would play Rue's keeper, not his liberator.

Lion told Rufus India'd come down from Halifax, was waiting downstairs. "Want to see her?"

Rue shook his head no. "I don't want her to see me shut up like some slave. Tell her I wish her... I wish her happiness."

What did Rufus want for his last meal? "Make it blueberry pie, Sheriff. A whole blueberry pie. I'll wash it down with two bottles of Sussex ginger ale."

Outside in the hot night, Salvation Army singers fountained voices like rosewater. Tambourines rustled like rivers.

George knew he'd never eat another Moir's chocolate. Now he wanted to be where he could breathe endlessly and see the sun eternally. Major Pretty and other members of the Fredericton Corps of the Salvation Army visited his cell. They composed a band whose members included Brothers Olds and Hoyt on trumpet and tambourine, Mrs. Hoyt, Omar Bird (feeling sorry for Rue), Mrs. Pretty, and James Synge on tambourine. They sang songs the death-empowered Georgie chose. The inmate even joined in at times on absurdly ecstatic harmonica. Everyone kept weeping while laughing, then laughing while weeping. Even the most calloused psalmist would never forget this night. Believers sang:

> *Why should Christian belief*
> *Shake and shiver like a leaf?*

George was so calm about his dying he was certain he wouldn't shame himself by pissing his pants when the rope wrung his neck. The moon rent the sky with light, shivering.

George'd been unfairly angry with Blondola for leaving the court when his cheating was exposed. But she'd still come to see him off. She'd brought Otho and Desiah. George just had tears coursing down his face and that of Blondola too. There were sobs, snuffles, flurries of the tissue paper Lion kindly provided. George told Blondola, bravely, his voice unbrave, "The Spirit of God was in my cell. I don't care anymore about the gallows."

Blondola was not mollified. "What about us, Joygee, yer babies an me?"

George just wept. "I'll be watchin over ya from above."

Blondola aimed fruitlessly for calm; Otho was looking like he wanted to cry and Desiah was wailing. She sobbed, "We was happy till Rue come out the pen. Rue's torn us down, ripped us apart. How'll we live, Joygee? How'll we live?"

George sobbed, "It weren't all Rue's fault. I was readin bad comics and gamblin and drinkin. I was a bad husband, a poor papa."

Blondola cried terribly, "You were *my* husband and *their* pa. We loved you just as you was, with all your silliness an sins, Georgie."

Then George handed Blondola a gift for the grown-up Otho: the silver-buckled belt Rue'd received from Easter. They hugged a last time. George asked, tenderly, "Blondola, how'd ya get that name? You've never said."

Blondola smiled through her tears. "Ma loved her blond Jesus, and she loved her dark Coca-Cola."

XIV

THE GALLOWS is winsome, awesome, lonesome, lithesome, elegant, functional, classically rough, and ultramodern. Standing on the platform in the barn, Ellis feels the strong, ripe rope; he feels the cool heads of the nails that lock it into place and make it strong enough to kill. Ellis wishes to touch the Hamiltons hardly, but gently. His violence against them must be an expert matter of rope, gravity, and their own weights, their own deeds, counting heavily against them. He pulls a lever that jets two bags of flour through the trap, tumbling, hanging. All is working fine.

George and Rue, chained at the neck, felt their flesh bruise from the weighty chain and heavy padlock each time one of them stumbled. Cool hands were about to grope their necks, crush their throats, while the approaching autopsy'd splay open their bellies. Calm, methodical Frederictonians'd wield stainless steel knives and scissors and cut up the boys' garb and nooses and hair. So only a last-minute British-inherited reserve would prevent their genitals from being sliced off and their skin stripped off for wallets and purses, as more excitable whites did to their black lynchees in the southern states.

The boys could not know that Alisha'd taken a train all the way from Three Mile Plains to Fredericton. She was the closest family of any sort they had left. She brought with her all the futile prayers—and effective prophecy—of Three and Five

Mile Plains. She camped out in the mob-filled streets in front of and around the prison, where, if it had rained, the vast numbers of bodies jostling and jockeying for the best vantage points to attempt to *feel*—for they could not witness—the imminent but closed-door execution of flesh-and-blood like themselves would've prevented any drop from moistening the ground.

Rufus, companioned by Bataille, and George, flanked by Pretty, walked from their cells, down stairs, and out the back of the jail to the small barn in its yard. The men now felt absurdly comfortable in the gently clanking chains on their wrists and ankles. During the brief seconds the brothers were visible to the massed, sandwich-and-pie-picnicking, beer-and-rum-guzzling hoi polloi outside the prison walls, a thunderous series of cheers erupted, punctuated by clapping and catcalls. Six local Klansmen milled about in white sheets and hoods with slits cut out for eyes.

A man's drunken voice shouted lustily, "Hang those black bastards! Or let us do it!" The crowd surged savagely, anticipating an orgiastic lynching, but the hundred cops round the jail pushed and clubbed the ringleaders back. But neither George nor Rue heeded the tidal attentiveness of their frothing audience. They vanished into the temporary refuge of the barn.

Sheriff Lion explained the final procedures and commanded the boys to bravery. (Both George and Rue felt calm. It wasn't hanging that was so bad, they reflected; it was the possibility of messing yourself that was disgusting.) All around the small, hay-strewn, shadow-busy barn, under a single electric light bulb, stood skull-faced police—witnesses—at attention. The atmosphere of the hanging barn was hot with hymns, muffled by the wood walls but still infiltrating the death chamber, turning it into some weird joint English-Latin, Protestant-Catholic service, with the Salvation Army band's marching music dovetailing with the Gregorian-like chants of the Eternal Church.

Ellis was poised funereally—a Gothic demon—atop the scaffold. The tolling church bells and the liquored-up shouts from the mob outside seemed quiet and far off now.

Sheriff Lion removed the chains from the Hamiltons. Without the extra weight, they felt light enough to fly. George turned and hugged Rufus. "I forgive you." That was Rufus speaking silently, George saying it aloud. Tears coated two fraternal faces. Then Lion tied the brothers' hands behind their backs and escorted them, shuffling, to the gallows staircase.

They scaled the mandatory thirteen steps to the top of the scaffold. There was no flinching, no nothing. The boys were so calm that some onlookers believed they'd been injected with morphine. But, no, their eerie, disturbing calm was that of Asa and Easter under water, that of Cynthy in that final bathroom. There was no point to feeling ill used or hard done by or disrespected: they could only pray agony would end in rapture. As soon as the sun'd first shone on them, it'd been shining on their graves. They knew it. Their stars were always a ceiling of nooses.

Ellis arranged the brothers on separate traps beside two nooses, belted their legs, affixed the ropes about their necks, and dropped black hoods over their faces. He was methodical, undistressed, and would have whistled, save that he enjoyed the gravity and solemnity of *professionally* administering death.

Outside the jail, a black hearse waited. A lightning-undiminished dark sparked above that jail as grey as *settecento* maps of the New World. A worrisome citizenry milled. A voice wailed, "Let's butcher em! Let's work em over!"

Rufus stood on the scaffold, his back to George, and lamented and rejoiced, all at once. He'd been dispensed no merciful love; now he was being dispensed with—mercifully. George imagined he'd laze on the edge of a cliff of gold where doves lie down, eat and drink to his heart's content.

The priest and the preacher opened their respective Bibles to speak final words of comfort and promise. They found it, strangely, hard.

Lion shouted "Uncover!" A dozen policemen-witnesses doffed their caps ceremoniously. Unceremoniously, Ellis yanked the lever that sent the trembling Hamiltons crashing down into eternity. George was in the middle of Psalm 23; Rufus was saying "Hail Mary" over and over again. The trap went *blam!* Just like that. As they fell, all the world swooped upwards like flowers. The brothers saw Asa, Cynthy, both forgiven, waiting for them just outside the barn. Rue could feel Easter next to him; George imagined he was holding Otho and Desiah and smiling at Blondola.

The masses in the hot, choking streets felt a collective spasm, a frisson, that made them gasp, quiver, vibrate in their genitals when they heard the trap violently clap, clatter, open. They felt emotionally alive now, but spent.

Was there a rich tremble, the double downslap of feet, a shaking of air and flesh? Two bodies braced like quail; they snapped to a stop, two feet off the floor. Then the stars were hanging, the heads of sunflowers were hanging, the ripening apples were hanging, and two minor Negroes were hanging where the Saint John River was drifting, drifting, drifting.

> *The boys were not hanged; they were felled.*
> *They were not conquered; they were quelled.*
> *Their deaths will last as long as life itself.*

The Negro hands of night moulded stars into immemorial, memorial pearls. *Finis the "Black Acadian" Tragedy of "George and Rue."*

CRYPT

The boys on the gully bridge
Rufus, George ...

—LORNA GOODISON

I

JULY 27, 1949, *Anno Domini:* the Hamiltons fell like dominoes. They merit no poetry, no laurels, no ballads, no statues, no headstones, no memory, no existence. They go the way of cats' and fishes' and horses' eyes.

The offspring of Three Mile Plains, Nova Scotia, is dry dust mixed in unmarked corners of two Fredericton cemeteries. The killers are better off as dirt. They be two crumbly chassis, two slushy torsos, all micked up with soil.

The Hamiltons sink in a damp cemetery, their sulking skeletons just blossoming along in soil laundered constantly by worms. They vegetate into carbon passing to oil before it crystallizes as diamonds. They'll be there always, springing snakes and ants and mushrooms and dead leaves and worms and weeds and soda pop bottles and cigarette lighters and marbles and soft, ripped-up newspapers.

IN DECEMBER 1949, just outside of Montreal, two men—Kenneth Bevin, seventeen, and Girvin Patenaude, nineteen—called a taxi driver, directed him out to the sticks, and, after driving about seven miles, hammered his head five times—making that indescribable sound that striking a hammer against a skull makes. They threw his corpse off a bridge into a murky river. The teens used the slain man's money to buy two boxes of shells, then they drove to a small town and robbed a bank with two .45 pistols that looked like bazookas. They took $5,000, and the cops found them the next night, asleep in a barn. They were sentenced to die. Ninety minutes before their hangings, word came their sentences'd been commuted to life in prison. George and Rue—black—had no such white luck.

India received Rue's letters three months after his death. She read and reread em. She wondered, "Can any word of Rue's live? Is a thought a body part?"

Barker's Point was demonized as Hammertown. Another nasty shenanigan exercised by downtown Fredericton society.

In Three Mile Plains, those who'd known the Hamiltons agreed to forget they'd ever been born, and to pour ink over their names in the registers where they'd been christened. Their only trace: yellowed, brittle newsprint.

NOTES

Did history really repeat itself?
Or only family history?

—BARBARA CHASE-RIBOUD

VERDICT

THIS NOVEL recapitulates bleakly truthful circumstances, but it is fiction, and I have taken prodigious
and relentless liberties with "facts," so that psycholo-
gies, identities, genealogies, and even some place descriptions
are purely imaginary. (But *History* is the truth, if you remember.)

Admittedly, the Hamiltons were my matrilineal first cousins
once removed; they died before I was born. I was innocent of
their existence—and their destruction—until May 1994, when
my mother commented, abruptly and briefly, on their homicide and their hangings.

Though repelled by the Hamiltons' crime, I embrace them as
my kin. They were born where I was born—in the Africadian
settlement of Three Mile Plains, Nova Scotia—and George
Hamilton and I were named for the same gentleman, his
grandfather and my great-grandfather, George Johnson. (In
naming me as she did, my mother salvaged the memory of that
perished cousin—and recuperated the regal name of her
grandfather.) Too, the Hamiltons were—like so many of us
from Three Mile Plains, Five Mile Plains, Windsor Plains (all
the same community, really)—part Mi'kmaq and part African.

Every heritage is coruscatingly complex. My other relatives
include contralto Portia White (1911–1968), filmmaker Sylvia
Hamilton (1950–), journalist William Clarke (1962–), and poet
Kirk Johnson (1973–). Ultimately, this novel conducts a tryst

with biography. Perhaps the dual impulse to creativity and violence in my own genealogy serves to illustrate the Manichaean dilemmas of the African odyssey in this strange American world.

George Elliott Clarke
(X. States)
Toronto, Ontario
Nisan IV

AFTER WORDS

THIS history of George and Rue was bred from original, monstrous truths. Still, I imbibed several works for atmosphere and accuracy: C. R. K. Allen, *A Naturalist's Notebook* (1987); Frank W. Anderson, *A Dance with Death* (1996); Robert L. Armstrong, ed., *Good Old Barker's Point* (1981); Velma Carter and Wanda Leffler Akili, *The Window of Our Memories* (1981), and Velma Carter and Leah Suzanne Carter, *The Window of Our Memories, Volume II* (1989); Dean Jobb, *Shades of Justice* (1988); and John Neal Phillips, *Running with Bonnie and Clyde* (1996). One passage in the novel adapts Basil Bunting's poem "The Orotava Road" (1935, 1950); another revisits Robert Browning's poem "How It Strikes a Contemporary" (1855).

The trial transcripts for George and Rufus Hamilton, as well as the letters both men wrote, are at the National Archives of Canada. Donald Harris gave me a typescript of *The Journal of George Hamilton* (1949) and copies of the Canadian Army medical and psychological assessments of George Hamilton.

This novel would not exist without the generosity of Harris, who met me at the Waterloo Hotel, in Waterloo, Ontario, on June 17, 1999, and shared with me his feelings and thoughts about the Hamiltons, their crime, and their executions. I am also indebted to the researches of my cousin and genealogist David "Skip" States. I thank Francis Nowacyznski for his dossier of bizarre crimes. At the National Archives, I also consulted the capital case records pertaining to the execution of Frank Rough-mond, for murder, in Stratford, Ontario, in 1905, as well as those respecting the 1950 murder trials of Kenneth Bevin and Girvin Patenaude in Quebec. At the New Brunswick Provincial Archives, I accessed stories carried by the Saint John *Telegraph-Journal* and the Fredericton *Daily Gleaner.* The Legislative Library of New Brunswick housed helpful press and Hansard records, and the Public Archives of New Brunswick furnished a host of photos. I benefited irreducibly from conversations or corre-spondence with Joe Blades, Hazen and Corinne Calabrese, Jerry Carty, Nancy Claybourne, James Elgee, Ruth Goodine, Sterling and Ann Gosman, Joan Harmon, Angus "Sock" Johnson, Cecil Johnson, Betty Lacey, Harley McGee, Bernice McIntyre, Lisa McLean, Bruce Oliver, Donald Parent, Jerome Peterson, Sarah Petite, Sue Rickards, Bill Scott, Patrick Toner, Thelma Walker, and Harold Wright. Michael Edwards of Science East in Freder-icton guided me on an exhaustive tour of the former York County Gaol. Eric J. Swinaker of the Legislative Library in Fredericton was unfailingly kind.

My editor, Iris Tupholme, was a steadfast seeker of excel-lence and, also, a paragon of patience. I would need to write another book to furnish adequate thanks and appreciation for her guidance. Copyeditor Shaun Oakey distinguished the pec-cadilloes from the peculiarities. My agent, Denise Bukowski, insisted, *for four years*, that I write—and finish—this novel! David Odhiambo eyed faults with forensic insight. Leilah Nadir's insistent enthusiasm for this story was uplifting. John Fraser was, as usual, irrefutably right about my wrongs. I also thank Noelle Zitzer for her positivist guidance. Kudos to Katie Hearn for her dextrous network management.

Austin Clarke, Alistair MacLeod, and Howard Norman, three great writers, granted me the charity of a hearing and the blessing of their endorsement. I thank them heartily—and with humility.

I accept total guilt for all errors and faults herein—as well as for my usage of Blackened English. These capital crimes are my own.

Thanks to the Rockefeller Foundation, the Banff Centre for the Arts, and the University of Toronto (especially Massey College) for financial—and time and space—aid.

I thank Geeta, my wife, for tolerating the time I put into this book. My art—despite its limitations—would not exist at all without Geeta's generous and instructive love.

Photo Credits: Public Archives of New Brunswick: overgrown shed (p. 3); car in flood (p. 113); and Mi'kmaq men with baskets (p. 153). Courtesy of George Elliott Clarke: Venetian grave (p. 211). National Archives of Canada: George Hamilton and Rufus Hamilton (p. 217).

George & Rue was written in Halifax, Nova Scotia; Ottawa, Ontario; Durham, North Carolina; Bellagio, Italy; Banff, Alberta; Toronto, Ontario; Venice, Italy; Vancouver, British Columbia; and Paris, France; 1994–2004.

www.randomhouse.co.uk/vintage